PONTIUS PILATE REFLECTS

by
Werner Koch

translated by
Edward Fitzgerald

SIMON AND SCHUSTER · NEW YORK · 1962

LIBRARY OF CONGRESS CATALOG CARD NUMBER: 62-9155
MANUFACTURED IN THE UNITED STATES OF AMERICA

PONTIUS PILATE REFLECTS

In re: VIIa-III-Ba

Herewith I submit a notarial inventory of
the items removed from the house of the
mentally deranged former Governor of the
Province of Judea, Pontius Pilate. Under
reference VIIb-III-Ba I append notes entitled by me "Pilate, Memoirs".

(Sig.) L. Pomponius Bassus
Notary

I

I⊤ was the night before last. I remember that I couldn't sleep. I was lying awake. There was a smell of decomposing flesh in the air, and the sky pressed down on the rooftops as though it were trying to stifle the whole of Rome. For weeks there had been no wind, and the streets were as though dead. I got up because I could get no air, and I went to the window. But outside it was even sultrier. Suddenly I thought that my wife had called out, and I went to see. But she was asleep. 'Ah well,' I thought. 'You were just mistaken.' Even when we were in Judea I had an idea that there was something wrong with my ears, but I didn't attach much importance to the matter at the time. When you're younger you don't take your body so seriously. I leant out of the window, looked up into the sky, wiped the sweat from my forehead, closed my eyes and fought for breath. But it was no use. Then I saw the cat.

I don't know how it got there. I certainly hadn't seen it before. It was dragging itself across the ground; crawling, head down. It would move along in this way for a while, and then it would stop, wait and listen. And then go on again; stop; and so on. And all the time it didn't really make much progress. Then it arched its back; its whole body seemed to contract, and after a moment or two like this, when it looked almost as though it were suspended in the air, it fell over as though it were dead.

9

I couldn't take my eyes off it. I would have liked to look away, up into the sky, or just straight ahead into the night, or simply close my eyes, but I couldn't. I just went on staring at the cat. 'Perhaps it will move again,' I thought. 'Nothing can just go suddenly stiff like that and die.' But it didn't move. I leant further out of the window. The street was dead, and I felt scared. The sweat on my forehead became colder and then drier. I looked round at my wife. She was asleep. Was she perhaps dead? Something or other, a human being, an animal or a movement of air must be there with her. No, I was the only one to see it, and I didn't even know if she had moaned. My hearing really wasn't very good any more; and apart from my wife no one knew how to talk to me. I didn't want to wake her up.

I looked out and down into the street, and I knew that this night there was nothing in the world but her and me. Her death and my dumb looking on. And we were both scared.

Suddenly the cat moved again. She crawled on her belly and dragged herself to the other side of the street. I could have helped her, but I just looked on. She moved by degrees to her death like a snail, apathetic, dragging herself through the dust of the street. As she reached the doorway I could hardly recognize her. Opposite in the house of Cassius everything was quiet. 'Perhaps she wants to die in the darkness,' I thought. Or perhaps she was just ill, or diseased, or exhausted by the heat. There are so many ways of being miserable. The heat was terrible.

It must have been at this moment that I stepped back from the window. My wife wakes up at the least noise, and now that I'm almost deaf I'm inclined to be a bit noisy. I lay down carefully and whispered:

"Are you there, Claudia?"

She remained silent. Whenever I wake up I always ask if she's there. It's become a habit. 'Let her sleep,' I thought. It doesn't matter whether she answers or not; the important thing to me is that I should have asked her. I envied her her ability to sleep. That hurts me now.

I lay awake. Was that cat scared perhaps? Did she prefer being in the shadow of the doorway? Perhaps she was dead already. I shouldn't like to die in front of Cassius's house. I should find it disagreeable. Were there perhaps cats which were deaf too? What would she be thinking about now? Did she know what dying meant? If she weren't in pain perhaps she was contented enough. Perhaps no one had ever bothered his head about her, and therefore she didn't mind much dying? But who bothers about us? And yet who doesn't care whether he lives or dies?

I was thinking too much. I always think too much. My thoughts are like tiny animals, small beetles with pointed legs running around inside my skull, dancing up and down, pricking, trampling around, here and there, up and down; restless beetle-like creatures who from time to time as though at a word of command rub their fore-legs against my brain and stridulate with high, clear notes—a great army of transparent thought insects with tiny voices. I try to get rid of them. I wash my head, immerse it in ice-cold water, squeeze my eyelids together, rub my forehead and beat my fists against my temples in order to hear nothing, never to hear anything again. But those little insects go on chirping. They find it amusing to whet their vibrating legs against my brain. They giggle. Their gibing laughter from a hundred thousand slavering throats scratches my skin, and claws right into it. My face screws up, and I can feel how distorted it is. 'Madness,' I think. Really, one day I might very well go mad; become an idiot staring at the world with dull eyes, and a few blackened stumps loose in a flabby mouth. No, not that!

I got up and went to the window. I couldn't sleep anyway. When I passed the back of my hand over my forehead, or wiped my eyes, the cold sweat suddenly became very hot and made me feel exhausted. I licked my lips, but they shrivelled up, burned and became very salty. Then I got scared, and everything burned more than ever. I felt worse and worse, and I called out to my wife again, but she didn't hear me. 'You must pull yourself together and let her sleep,' I thought.

I thought of the cat again. What for? Whether she was dead or alive, whether she was scared, whether she died apathetically, or perished of thirst in the heat—what did that matter to me? I had a headache. I thought that at any moment the veins in my forehead were going to burst, and then ooze out as though a boil had been lanced. Would it perhaps do any good if I suddenly knocked my head against the wall? No, that wouldn't help; on the contrary it would probably make matters worse. No, the thing to do was to keep quite still—and think of something else. Think of anything. Think of Claudia, for instance. Or of a storm, a storm of ice-cold rain. I had to keep swallowing, but there was really nothing there to swallow any more. My saliva had dried up. 'Actually you love your wife,' I thought. That made me a bit calmer to-day, because I really thought that; I wasn't just deceiving myself.

I can't imagine what would have happened to me without my wife. I should never have become anything at all, and certainly not Governor. I should have spent my whole life along the Tiber, staring at the water, watching the rings the fish make when they snap, wasting my time, and perhaps letting my mind run on. In the best case I might have become a teacher, or an actor perhaps. They say there's not much money in either of those lines, but I really don't attach a great deal of importance to money —and still less to titles, public reputation and glory. And I'm not saying that because I was removed from my post either. There were quite different reasons for that, and I don't want to set myself up as the judge. I don't know whether I was a good Governor and a bad man, or a good man and a bad Governor. One thing is quite certain: you can't be both together. I, Pontius Pilate, always stood at the Governor's side. I didn't like him much, and for the most part I rather despised him too. We were two different people, and we had different views. We didn't get on very well, and sometimes we didn't know what to do for the best.

But all that's not to the point now.

My headache was almost intolerable. The moment I moved—perhaps my arm, my little finger, or even my head—I could feel those insects scrabbling around inside my brain. For two pins I would have shrieked out loud. I couldn't stand it any longer. Finally there was absolutely nothing left but the one idea: I must wake up my wife. She would help me.

What happened after that I don't know. All I know is that she's dead.

And there are moments when I know it with terrible certainty.

13

II

I TELL myself that I meant well when I didn't want to wake her up. But no matter how often I say it, it doesn't help much. Perhaps she cried, or moaned, or called my name before she died? Perhaps she wanted a drink of water? Perhaps she would still be alive if . . . I didn't hear anything. I was standing at the window, feeling miserable, and bothering about a cat. When I finally went to her to wake her up because I was miserable, she looked at me with great eyes. I noticed at once that they were too large. They were fixed and glassy, and yet full of wonder. They didn't understand me. I was a mystery to them. And that look is haunting me, and I torment myself ceaselessly. There I was at the window looking up into the sky, looking out into the night, looking at the cat, turned away from her; and she dies; the begging lips, the slow dropping of the head, the eyes gradually opening to the last wide stare.

And all she saw was my back, my hunched shoulders. And I blocked out the sky for her. At what moment did she die? Had the cat managed to get to Cassius's by that time? Had she really called me? Was she perhaps already dead when I lay down beside her and whispered, "Are you there?" No, not that!

I talked to her far too little. I was fond of her, but I should have told her so. There's a lot I've got to make up for, but how do you do that when there's only a grave ahead of you? She was always so cheerful, and people thought she was really rather frivolous. But they thought that only because they didn't really know her. When I was still Governor I managed to stand it only because of her. She could sit in a corner and weep quietly, but she did that only when she was alone. As soon as I came she would wipe her tears away quickly; and then she had gentle, trusting eyes, and she would smile at me. She would think I hadn't noticed anything, but I certainly had. I just didn't say anything, that was all. On one occasion I was trying someone, and she was quite convinced that he was innocent. And there and then in the middle of the trial she had a note passed to me begging me to be very careful just this time. I was rather annoyed at the incident because I was always careful and I always tried to be just. I can't remember the details very clearly any more. All the same, I don't know what I would have done without her.

I ought to know it now. But I don't want to. I chat to her, look towards the door, wait until it opens (it opens for me) and then I say: "Have you been into town?" "It's raining," she says. "You haven't caught cold, have you?" I ask. "Take care of yourself." And then we fall silent because I can't make conversation. But I brace myself, look at her, and want to say: "You know I'm very fond of you." But I can't bring myself to. The words won't come over my lips. I think to myself: 'I'm very fond of you, you know', and my lips move, but because I don't say anything she asks: "Have you got a headache?" "No, that's all right; don't worry," I reply. "You ought to take a walk," she says. "No, I'd sooner stay here with you," I answer.

Afterwards, when I grasp it again it's all more difficult.

As though she would die again and again. But I want her with me at least once a day. But why, why did I remain silent all that time?

My headaches are becoming worse. When one starts I darken the room, sit down in the corner and wait. sometimes I sit there half the day, just like that with my eyes closed, and my hands folded, waiting. I can hear my breath coming and going; I could go to sleep or die. And rats gnaw at the inside of my skull. I want to shake them off, but then they hold on tighter than ever. And I wait. She always said we should die together.

III

Now my father was a man who knew how to live. But how do you *know* a thing like that? He hadn't the faintest idea why he lived; but there, he didn't care either; he just wasn't interested. "Why do hens lay eggs?" he would ask, and answer: "Because the eggs taste good." He found that very funny.

I never got on very well with him. He was an advocate, and he had a very good practice and many friends. "Make a note of that, boy," he would say to me. "Never make enemies. Be polite to everyone; in fact be friendly to everyone; and whatever you do, don't offend anyone. That's the only way you'll get anywhere. *Think* the truth if you like, but keep it to yourself; no one wants to hear it. And whatever you do, don't cause me any trouble."

I can hear him now.

I did cause him trouble though.

He had very rich clients: whores from the best society and priests of good family. He wasn't particular, and he didn't mind whether his clients were in the right or not. He wasn't even interested. Though, of course, to have lots of money and be in the right was an ideal case. To have lots of money and have something in your favour was all right too. But the thing which really stimulated him was when his client had lots of money and was completely in the wrong. To be in the right and to have no money didn't interest him in the least.

He was a highly respected man, and he attached great importance to knowing the right people—even if they were even more stupid than they were boring. And as for a Senator, that was the highest desideratum. "We're invited to Senator so and so," he would say, and from the tone of his voice you knew that he really meant "You see what an important man I am?"

I don't know what brings it into my mind at the moment, but a few years before I was recalled I was talking to a criminal. It was at my country place in Caesarea, and the fellow must have been lying in wait for me. My servants knew him quite well. He was a Jew, and he had some sort of post in some sort of party. He was a fanatic, of some sort, and he wanted to "Lead" Judea, or "Free" Judea, it doesn't matter which; I can't quite remember any more. One evening I came across him in my garden and I took him into my study to question him. It appeared that his name was Barabbas. He was a short, stocky fellow, and I should have guessed him to be some sort of publican rather than a fighter for freedom. My guards were astonished when I took him into the house. However, the thing amused me.

I invited him to sit down, offered him a drink, and quite generally treated him as one would an invited guest. He hadn't expected that, of course, and he was flabbergasted. He just stood there and stared at me. Of course, there's nothing new in these big-mouthed agitators having nothing to say for themselves when they find themselves face to face with their enemies, but I must say that his complete confusion surprised me a little. However, I was determined to make him talk. I began by asking him why he had apparently been lying in wait for me? Did he intend to kill me?

He made no answer. Just stared at me as though I were something uncanny. Perhaps he had imagined me a very different person; thought I would be a barbarian or a brute perhaps. He was rather undersized himself and perhaps forty years old. I noticed in particular that he had very short fingers. He seemed aware of it too, for he was obviously anxious to hide them. However, there was something strangely agile about him and I could imagine that as a spouter he might well sway a mob audience. I asked him whether he hated me personally, or what it was all about.

He still stared at me silently, but then he suddenly said: "We are all of us against Rome, and that means against you too."

He spoke far too loud and he spoke with a strong provincial dialect. I knew that he must have said just that sort of thing a hundred times before he found himself saying it to me. But I was a little surprised at his courage.

I looked at him, but my glance told him nothing. Then I asked " 'We' are all against Rome? Who's 'we'? Are there many of you then?"

18

Now he looked at me smugly with his piglike little eyes and said boastfully: "All of us; that's right. That means me and my followers."

"So you have followers?"

"Of course."

"And you're all against me?"

"Yes, all of us."

But now he avoided my eyes, became more and more nervous, and his hands clenched and unclenched nervously. It was easy enough to see that he already regretted his courage and was scared. He found it difficult to look me in the face. Now and again he squinted towards me out of the corner of his eyes, and the longer I remained silent the more nervous he became. But I wanted to get more out of him; what he had to say might come in useful.

"I take it that you didn't come here just to find some opportunity to tell me that?"

At that he looked at me, bent forward, with his hands on his knees, as though he were making a great revelation, and then said almost condescendingly:

"You once helped me, and now I want to help you. Barabbas is a man who knows what's the right thing to do. That goes without saying, and we needn't discuss it. Politically, of course, we are enemies, but humanly speaking . . ." And he went on in this rather stilted fashion for a while, finally telling me that an attempt was being planned on my life and that he had come to warn me.

Needless to say, I wasn't taken in for one moment. How should I have helped him? And if an attempt were really being planned on my life, why would he of all people come to warn me of it? However, I made no comment and went on as though I were not interested in the matter. What had I done to help him? I asked.

The question was a trifle disconcerting, I could see. He was a leader of the people, and thus a man whom one ought to know. My ignorance was therefore an insult. Like so many others of his kidney, he took it for granted that everyone must know him and remember the details of his trial, but I'm afraid I couldn't. For him it was *his* trial; for me it was just a trial. You get used to that sort of thing. But then he mentioned the name of a man who had played a certain role in the disturbances and confusions of those days, and after that I began to remember who the fellow before me was. Sometimes you need only a very little stimulus, a word, or a movement of the hand, in order to remember some happening that has temporarily escaped your mind. The trial of the man Jesus, in which this fellow Barabbas was implicated, had remained in my mind because of a disagreeable dream my wife had had in connection with it. It made such an impression on her that she would recall it even months afterwards. She was very sensitive to anything mysterious, and sometimes, when she was particularly cheerful . . . But let me get back to my interview with Barabbas.

He advised me to leave Judea altogether, or at least to keep my whereabouts a secret. I just looked at him and said nothing. I wanted to shake his confidence and make him uncertain.

"Oh, yes," I said finally. "An attempt on my life. I know all about that."

I could see that he didn't believe me. Was he really a criminal, I wondered. As he sat before me, a little doubtfully, but eager to be helpful, he didn't particularly look like one. I told him that there was nothing I was

20

afraid of. I had ruled the country justly, maintained law and order as it was my duty to do, and always taken the wishes of his political friends into consideration as far as possible. What point was there in assassinating me therefore? Nothing would be gained thereby; on the contrary. The new Governor would have a different name, but would that make any difference? Would he be any better, for example? And the Roman State would not be at a loss either to deal with the murderers or to appoint a successor. So what would they gain by disposing of me?

A man must not become the slave of his slaves.

IV

IT occurred to me that there was rather more to it than appeared on the surface. If I am not mistaken, at the time Barabbas was tried he was a strong, tough fellow. My soldiers reported that he had sung seditious songs in his cell and had tried to joke with the warders. The idea that a murderer—Barabbas had killed a rich Syrian merchant—is always naturally cold and without feeling is quite wrong. Of course, at the moment when they commit the deed murderers do have an icy, inhuman heart. What they do is a bestial thing, and thus they obviously have bestial urges. But when their own lives are at stake they usually sing a different tune; they become incredibly flabby and shameless; they have no dignity, they weep and moan, where formerly... (What do I mean by that? *Formerly?* I mean when she was alive of course:

I wake up, come to, rub my eyes, look over to her, stretch out my arm, put my hand on her shoulder and whisper "Are you there?" And then I think: 'She's there, and now you can go on dreaming and lying there peacefully.')

Formerly I used to say to her: "My murderers all look like young girls." She didn't much care for such jokes. And now I don't either. Incidentally, it's not a complete invention. When a murderer is brought before the court he's usually feeling very sorry for himself. You'd think to look at him that he wouldn't harm a fly; and some of them are worse than cowards. It is right, of course, that people who kill other people should themselves die, but the execution of the sentence isn't everything. Merely to bring home a man's crime to him and then to pass judgment isn't all. When I have a man executed there is necessarily a relationship between him and me; but not only between him and me—also between his wife and me; between his mother and me; between his brother and me . . . I have caused the man, the husband, the son and the brother to be executed. And if the mother loses her reason because she loses her son where do I stand in the affair?

I have often been told that I have a foolish tendency to indulge in pointless ideas. Though, of course, nowadays no one says anything at all to me. My old friends are either dead or they don't want to know me any more—though it's true that some of the more simple gentlemen do just greet me hastily on the street. But even they take good care that no one sees them.

But I don't make my thoughts. They come to me on their own; and, after all, it's I who have to wrestle with them. I have gradually come to certain conclusions which I prefer to keep to myself because I don't care to expose myself to public derision. But all the same I feel very strongly about them. For example, in my view it would be a good thing if all judges had not only to give the reasons for their death sentences, but also to carry them out. Beyond all question that would make a very big difference. Just think: supposing I had to lift the stone, without trembling, keeping my eye on the victim's head, and then strike hard and true. Take a nail and drive it through the centre of the palm, on a level with the base of the thumb, where the skin grows white. Force the hand to keep still, put the point of the nail at the right spot, measure my stroke, pause a moment to make quite certain perhaps, then strike. Hear the scream; wait without excitement; watch the blood running; strike again; make sure that the hand doesn't wrench itself away. Watch the hand shudder, watch it convulse; see the fingers closing and the finger-nails digging into the flesh, succeeding only in making the wound worse. And then the other hand. Just the same procedure again. Gag the man, shout at him, kick him, bang his head against the wood to keep him quiet. Another nail. The second hand more obstinate perhaps, closing frantically to a bloodless white fist, desperately striving to put off the moment of death. But the job has to be finished. Seize the fist therefore, wrench the fingers apart, force the hand back into position, drive the nail in: dripping blood again, jerkings, shrieking; a knee in the belly. "Shut up, you swine!" Drinking companions below, a frantic woman tries to get at me, soldiers drag her back. Where is that damned nail? The head drops. The eyes of the dying man see me through swirling mist a few inches away; they take me in, without hatred. But I'm too late. Blast it! The feet, the nails, blood. Where do I drive the nails in now? The hands are fairly easy; they're just made as though to drive nails through. One good blow is enough. The feet now, that's much more difficult.

Every judge should be compelled to face that situation. Now that really would be a good law. Whoever condemns a man to death does so not only with understanding and conviction, but with his whole being, physical as well as mental. How often does it happen in our times that a man is put out of the way for political and not moral considerations! In such cases it is ridiculous to leave the execution of the sentence to ordinary professional executioners. They have no idea of the difference between morality and politics, and they have ten times more in common with any condemned man than with all the judges in Rome. Our younger judges are too casual.

But I've got away from Barabbas again. I don't usually let myself be carried on from idea to idea like this; on the contrary, I have a tendency to get bogged down in one groove. But now, when I'm forcing myself to write down something just because it happens to be going through my mind and because it helps me to keep my mind off other things—I don't want to think of my wife—I'm beginning to wonder what Barabbas has got to do with me. What do I care about him? Why am I bothering my head with him? Who is Barabbas, anyway? And for that matter: who am I? A discussion between a murderer and a Governor—is that particularly interesting? Perhaps it is. But what's the point?

He had certainly changed physically. When he was brought to trial he was a solid fellow, powerful, and with a head like a bullet and the neck of a bull. His eyes looked away beyond the people in court; they weren't important enough for him. He stood there with his feet apart as though rooted to the ground, and he didn't even bother to look at me. He wasn't afraid. He didn't seem to know what fear was. He would have been a good man for the army, but he didn't like our army. He made quite a favourable impression on me.

But later on, at the time of my discussion with him, you would hardly have recognized him. He gave me the impression that somehow he had got smaller; his face was puffy, his eyes were muddy and restless, his hands were podgy. He didn't look like a hero any more, but like some sort of very ordinary minor official perhaps. His fighting days seemed to be over and he made no more rabble-rousing speeches. He had become respectable, and he lived on the past. He read reports of the raids he had once directed, and he made marginal jottings. He had forgotten that hunger was unpleasant, that thirst makes you exhausted, and that the shedding of blood satisfies.

But his impertinence was getting on my nerves now, and I didn't feel inclined to listen to the rubbish any longer.

"Believe me," he insisted urgently, "bigger things are at stake. I was on Golgotha when it happened. I wanted to have a look at the thing for once; and in particular I wanted to see how he would take it. So I saw it myself. And the heavens darkened."

"Really?" I said casually.

"Yes, and the Temple curtain was rent. I didn't believe that, of course, but then I saw it with my own eyes. They say that he didn't die at all, and that afterwards his tomb was empty. And you should have seen the stone they rolled in front of it! Five of your strongest men couldn't have shifted it. Really, it would be a good thing for you if you . . ."

When I asked him who he was talking about he mentioned the name Jesus. It was that of a man I had sentenced to be crucified at the time. Barabbas really seemed to believe that there was something out of the ordinary about this man. It is very often difficult for the head of any occupying power to find his way around in the opinions and feelings of the natives. They are foreigners as far as we are concerned; they hate us; and in their eyes I was some sort of villain rather than a man. They certainly wouldn't believe that I'm just an ordinary human being, that I'm very fond of my wife, that I often get up early in the morning to see the sun rise, that I suffer from headaches, that I'm a bit hard of hearing, and that I read Seneca. They also wouldn't believe that I couldn't kill a chicken, because to see its body twitching afterwards would upset me too much. For them I just have to be a cold-hearted villain, and a cruel brute, personally responsible for all the atrocities of the Roman Empire; not a human being at all, but an organ of the State: cold, lifeless, inhuman and godless.

But that's not the way I am at all.

I haven't a headache at the moment.

V

ALL my life I haven't been very kind. I could, of course, excuse myself by saying that, apart from my wife, no one has ever been very kind to me either, but that really wouldn't be the reason. I never knew my mother. All I know is that the many acquaintances and supposed friends of my father, and the visitors, never mentioned her. In our house it was a matter of good taste never to say anything about her. Nevertheless, I knew almost all there was to know. I grew up without anyone's having kissed me good night, or stroked my head fondly. And if I happened to wake up at night I would always hear the sound of drunken voices bawling, my father shouting, and the giggling and laughter of cheap women. I would lie awake and weep. The tears grew cold on my cheeks and formed a dry crust. I called out, got up and called out again, crying, drumming on the wall. . . . But my father had a party and no one heard me. My father talked in a loud voice, bursting into laughter, bellowing like some beast in heat and trampling around. I was afraid, and as I wept I cried: "Father! Father! I'm crying. I'm frightened. What are you laughing at? Why don't you ever come to me. I want to love you. I will love you if you come right now. Please come."

I stood there and waited, listening. My feet got cold. But my father wasn't thinking of me. A woman's voice shrieked. 'I wonder what he's doing to her?' I thought. 'It sounds as though he's killing her. But why is she laughing if he's going to kill her? Grown-ups seem to have ununderstandable ideas. And no heart. I stood there alone: with my thoughts, with my tears, with my fear. Would it do any good if I jumped out of the window? That was an idea. That would stop my father laughing! Yes, I wanted to jump out of the window and hit my head on the pavement and lie there motionless, stiff and silent. My father would have to bother about me then. Perhaps he would even weep himself. I should have liked that. I got up again, looked out of the window, and thought about what would happen if I really did it. But then I thought: 'Nothing at all will happen. He'll just go on laughing. And his friends will go on laughing. Those women will go on laughing. Everyone will just go on laughing. And I'll just lie there on the street with blood all over my head. A lot of blood. And when I'm dead and stiff, and they come out and notice me, it will be too late. They certainly won't notice anything until they've stopped laughing anyway. But then they'll be tired, and strangely quiet, and the sky will be getting lighter. But when they find me at last it will be too late. I shan't need them any more.' All I wanted was that they should stop laughing. But there was no way I could make them stop; no way at all. And the women were the worst. Women laugh differently, I thought then. I didn't like any of them. They had such wide mouths, and when they kissed me I didn't like the taste of their lips either. I went back to bed. I wanted to sleep. The tears had dried in ridges on my cheeks and my face was sticky.

My mother?

I was just two years old when she was executed. My father, who was already a well-known advocate at the time, had caught her keeping a tryst with a slave. He wasn't anxious to follow the thing up; he was thinking of his practice and his reputation. But in the end the whole thing came out. In order to avoid being executed my mother opened the veins in her wrists, but the attempt was unsuccessful. My father nursed her well again. They must have become reconciled soon after that. In any case, the affair never became public.

But it wasn't long before she was publicly accused, against the will of my father, of professional procuring. My father did his utmost to save her, but all his oratorical

arts were in vain. I don't think he loved her. As far as
he was concerned the whole business was just another
"case", embarrassing and very bad for his reputation and
his practice. He was willing to pay several thousand
denarii in bribes, but the judges refused—not because
they were incorruptible but because the Emperor himself
was sufficiently interested in the case to have reports of
it laid before him. And who would dare to risk the dis-
pleasure of the Emperor?

My father was a brilliant orator, for he did not believe
a word he said. When he was present in court for important cases he would wear borrowed rings in order to
impress the spectators; and any case in which there was
anything to be earned was good enough for him. He was
prepared to defend anything, as long as there was money
in it for him. I remember (I think very likely this was the
first incident I ever remembered) his coming back to the
house and telling my governess that he had just succeeded
in getting several thousand denarii out of the very rich
Theocritus. He didn't know Theocritus very well, but
he managed it, and on the old man's death-bed too. He
was able to talk so persuasively that the living and the
dying would give way to him and promise him everything. I inherited nothing of that talent.

Years ago I sentenced someone to death because the
mob demanded it. Of course one ought not to take any
notice of the mob, but it's easy to say that. I even declared
publicly that the verdict had been forced on me, and what
was the result? The mob merely concluded that if Pilate
washed his hands in innocence like that he must be weak,
helpless, and without power. But all the time I was
merely being honest. Dare a man still be honest? Are there
things which are worth more than money, title, fame?

Will this world end one day? The Greeks were wise, they tell us; they had a Socrates. But what use was that to them? Most Romans regard Socrates as a silly fellow, and my neighbour Cassius as a demi-god. And the difference? Socrates calmly and serenely drinks the hemlock, whilst Cassius gives uproarious carousals. I live opposite him, look out on to the street. The night is bright, particularly on that dark patch of ground where the cat began to die. I can see its fear, its convulsions. It is still night, and in the house of Cassius the "quality", the new rich, the profiteers and the wasters are all there; for Cassius is a friend of the Emperor's. So what? What is an Emperor? What is Cassius? And what are they?

If Claudia were still alive she would be sleeping now. She would be lying beside me, and I would stretch out my hand to her and whisper: "Are you there?" I would take her hand and hold it in mine and tell her "I love you". But it's too late for that now. You love what you haven't got any more.

VI

FOR the first time after that I went into town. I don't feel at home there any more. I was hardly on the street when I felt giddy. I closed my eyes and leaned against the wall of a house and waited until the fit passed. I'm no longer used to going out. When the dizziness had gone and I opened my eyes again I found myself looking at the spot where the cat had lain. I was standing quite close to it, and I looked at it again and again. At first I couldn't move, but then it drew me over against myself. I bent down and examined the ground, imagining perhaps that I should find something or other: cat's hairs, a drop of blood, or the marks of her paws. A beetle crawled by rapidly, obviously in a tremendous hurry. I had just straightened myself and was going over towards the door of Cassius's house to see if there were any traces there when suddenly Stephanio stood beside me and greeted me.

He quite startled me. I hadn't seen him come up, and since I have been back from Judea I find myself subject to sudden attacks of anxiety. Of course that's connected somehow with my deafness. Sometimes I feel as though there's someone behind my back. I haven't seen or heard anything, but I feel frightened; and I turn round slowly, only to find that there's no one there after all.

Stephanio has grown old. Since he's no longer on the stage most people have forgotten him; and a good many of those people who haven't forgotten him avoid him. We went into town together. He tried to start a conversation with me, but he soon noticed that I didn't hear what he was saying. I can usually read the other fellow's face and tell when the time comes to nod and agree with him, but Stephanio's face is lifeless; it doesn't give any inkling of what he is thinking. It was only when he asked me how my wife was that my ears were unusually keen for a moment. I heard his question very clearly, and I looked at him carefully. 'No,' I thought, 'he really hasn't heard she's dead.' And then I started talking to him quickly about foolish, nonsensical things. Perhaps there's something wrong with my head as well as my hearing? "Ah, yes," I said. "It's nice of you to inquire. She's very well, thank you. She isn't troubled so much with her gall stones now", which was certainly true. And then! "Oh, that? No we didn't mind my being recalled at all. On the contrary." Yes, we did live a very retired life, but we got on well together; and that was, of course, the main thing. "Everything's quite all right, thank you."

When we said good-bye he smiled, saying he had to go because he'd been invited by this or that Senator, I forget which one, but it was a very important invitation I remember. The details escape me. Of course, he was lying, just as I was. His fame was a thing of the past, and people had already forgotten it—and him. That's the way it is in the theatre; they soon forget you. And he was good, mark you. I can remember very clearly how the audiences used to applaud him. I saw him in several pieces, and I must say that I was quite impressed. But that's all over now. Who knows him to-day? All right, but why does he have to pretend to me? Why does he have to lie to me? Although, of course, he may just have wanted some excuse to get rid of me. After all, what's a dismissed Governor? Not the most useful kind of acquaintance. There's not much profit, and even a certain danger, in being seen in his company. And then, over and above that, a deaf old man who only wants to talk about his dead wife isn't a very lively companion.

In any case, perhaps I didn't even understand what he said. It was all very vague.

I no longer seem to find my way around easily. The whole world collects in this town. I could hardly get along. The people were swarming all over the streets, an endless moving column of strange faces with moving lips. They crowd in front of the displays, look into the shops and admire the goods set out: Spanish wool,

Chinese silk, coloured glasses from Alexandria, rare wines, oysters from Greece, herbs from Africa, emeralds from the Urals, perfumes from Arabia. It's really astonishing how prosperous we are, or seem to be. A thousand people stand around, buying, examining, bargaining, or going off with packages, bolts of cloth, and other purchases. And children galore, some of them lost and crying for their mothers, and being jostled and pushed around. I was carried along with the crowd and couldn't get out again; just swept along as the mob decreed: rich men, slaves, coloured men, thieves, tramps, corner boys, gapers; the whole world seemed on its feet, making its way through the streets of Rome. All I could hear was a dull, soughing sound; my ears were refusing their service. But my eyes could see babbling lips, jerky movements, people calling out, people passing on rumours, people gesticulating. There was an animal trainer making his bear dance clumsily. A man who said he was a ship-wrecked sailor was holding a lump of timber in his hands and asking for alms, running after people, telling them that his ship had gone down, and that this was the boat-hook he had rescued—the boathook! All he had managed to save! Look at it, smell it! It smells of the sea, doesn't it? Salty. And I'm all alone with what I stand up in. Have pity on me. Give me money, please. I had the impression that he was lying. You could see that, I thought.

A laden animal forced its way through the crowds, and people protested indignantly, cursing the animal, its owner, and the world in general. Astonishing how much they find to complain about. A hunchback was offering cloth for sale. He seized a passing woman by her skirt so that she should stop and look at his goods, but the woman was unwilling even to look. Young louts cat-called, and pestered the girls. I spotted a small boy stealing a bracelet, and I was just going to shout out "Stop thief!" when it suddenly occurred to me that it was no business of mine. All I wanted was to get out of the crowd, to get away from this pressing, shoving, anonymous colossus, but it was no good; I couldn't get away. There I was and I had to go where I was carried.

It grew dark, but there were still just as many people as before; moving forward, pushing and shoving. Each one a human being like myself. But what did that matter? What was important was the flesh and blood, the strength of the muscles, the ruthless drive, the determined will. That's the sort of thing that counts. I wondered what they were all thinking about. And what would happen in the end. What would happen when all the shops were empty and all the money was gone? What would come after the sale? They would go on pushing, that was certain. But what for? If they went on pushing and shoving, fighting for a better place and abusing each other after all the shops were empty; what would happen then? When there were no more scents, no more precious stones, and no more hot sausages? They had some excuse for all their pushing and shoving now: they wanted a hot sausage, or something quite different perhaps. But anyway it was there. But what when one day they forced their way to the front and found nothing there for them? What then?

One drawback of writing like this is that it brings on my headaches. But if I don't write I find myself thinking about Claudia, and I don't want that. It reminds me that she's dead, and I don't like that either.

VII

I was pushed and carried along with the crowds, and although several times I did my best to get free I didn't succeed; I was swept along regardless of my own wishes in the matter. In the end I resigned myself to it. You get used to such things, and the sooner the better when there's nothing else you can do. Sometimes I even had a rather agreeable feeling that I had gone under; that I was no longer there; that no one knew me; that no one was taking any notice of me. And, above all, that no one knew that I was Pontius Pilate; and that suited me.

It was dark now, and I began to wonder how I was going to get home. And then a very different movement ran through the crowd, something like a sudden jolt. I was pushed to one side; people started shouting; someone even shouted at me. But I didn't understand what he said. Sometimes I lost my footing altogether, and I was carried along like that without touching the ground at all. And the others jabbered away to each other, forced their way forward, abused each other, and pointed at something. And then I spotted it—a fire! It's not so long ago that they increased the strength of the Fire Brigade by seven thousand men. But what good did that do? First of all they always came too late, and even when they do come fairly soon the mob just won't let them through— they want to see the fire, and they don't want to lose their places.

I suppose about a hundred houses were burning. The air was thick with smoke and soot, and there was a sweetish, pungent smell. I was still being carried along by the mob of sightseers. Then I saw a very old man with long, white hair. He was covering his head and face with his arms and hands so that I could see only his nose and a pair of beady, glistening eyes. He was bending over a charred, shrivelled and blackened body. I'll swear the head was no bigger than a fist. Only the mouth was large, and that was wide open. The legs stuck into the air like rusty iron hooks. The old man was kneeling over the disfigured face and a few tears fell from his eyes. It was a horrible sight, and I closed my eyes to shut it out. Just be carried on. In the still glowing ashes of one house a girl was screaming and dancing. She had torn off her clothes, and she was trampling around in the embers like a mad woman, flinging up her arms and singing and shouting. Then suddenly she collapsed and lay still.

I found it difficult to breathe now. My mouth was wide open like a fish in an effort to pump more air into my lungs, but the whole air was full of smoke, and that made it worse. I found myself suddenly sweating over my whole body, and then immediately afterwards I began to shiver. I had only one thought now: how to work my way out of this mob. I tried to elbow my way out vigorously, but that only made them irritable. A man even punched me in the stomach, and a young man kicked me. After that I gave up. I didn't care any more. 'Let them do what they like,' I thought; 'it really doesn't matter.' So I just closed my eyes. I felt very wretched, and I made no further resistance; just let myself be carried along. They were still grumbling about me, but I didn't bother. 'Do whatever you like,' I thought.

It was just before midnight when I finally got back. Eleazar had obviously been worrying but he said nothing. I went into Claudia's room, sat down and started to think about nothing in particular. There was still a smell of her scent in the room. I would have liked to weep, but I was too exhausted even for that.

VIII

YESTERDAY when I was dressing: Eleazar has been with me almost twenty years now and it occurred to me that he knew me better than I knew myself.

"Would you like to be free, Eleazar?" I asked.

"No," he replied bluntly.

"But it would be better for you to be your own master, Eleazar, wouldn't it?"

"No," he repeated.

He didn't want to be anything but what he was, but surely everyone wants to be something more, something better, something more famous; in short something different from what he is? One might want to be a poet, the other an actor, the third a Senator. And this one even an Emperor. What made him so different from other people then? So I asked him.

No, he said, he didn't think he was so very different from other people. Did I want to know his opinion? He would write it down for me: "No living thing ever wants to change with any other." That surprised me. Surely, I insisted, he would sooner be an advocate, or a

doctor, or perhaps Pilate, or something else altogether?
No.

But as Stephanio the people would clap and cheer him in the theatre, I pointed out. As Cassius he would be the lord and master of four hundred slaves; with a wonderful house and as much money as ever he wanted so that he could give parties and banquets every day. Every doctor, every advocate was a free man, with a house, an income, a wife, a family. And the Emperor controlled the world. Even I must seem an enviable man to him since I gave the orders and he had to obey them.

No.

He looked at me, and he was obviously a little embarrassed. He smiled placatorily and shook his head. I told him to write down what he had to say against my point of view, and he wrote: "Stephanio is not a good man. Cassius has to intrigue for the Emperor's favour. Advocates deceive their clients. Doctors can't help theirs. The Emperor takes the lives of others. Pilate has no wife any more. But I still remain Eleazar."

The thing interested me, and I searched in my mind for something to refute his case, but I couldn't think of anything at all. It's clear enough, I suppose, that a man under sentence of death would willingly change places with anyone, but that really isn't much of an argument because he isn't making a free choice but merely adopting a desperate expedient in order to stay alive. In any case, as far as I was concerned I didn't want to change with anyone else either. And it wasn't that I was all that satisfied with my own skin. Perhaps the yoked oxen, beaten and goaded day after day, would sooner be a peasant. Perhaps. But who knows? How did you calculate the profit and loss at the end of the day? Would the beggar really prefer to be a philosopher? If he were he would have to live even more frugally; and he'd get a great deal less sleep. Would I, for example, like to be in power and influence again? Perhaps I would. But for that I should have to slip into the skin of my successor, and I can't say I really like the fellow. Furthermore, he has a very nasty son who has gone to the dogs completely, and I shouldn't care for that. Would I like to be Cassius then? No. Or B.? No, B. is stupid. A. then? No, A. bows and scrapes to the Emperor and deceives him behind his back. But perhaps I should have liked to be a Socrates? No, because in that case I should never have got to know my wife at all; and they would have killed me . . .

Eleazar was right. I preferred to remain Pilate.

But was there any satisfaction or consolation in that?

IX

P. WAS a man of fifty-six and he lived in Rome. As a proconsul in the colonies he had got to know foreign parts and strange peoples; and he had always done what he thought to be his duty. But favour and disfavour are separated by a hair's breadth, so although he had done nothing wrong P. was removed from his post. In the years that followed his dismissal he kept himself more and more away from social life. He had an idea that people were inclined to avoid him, and that primarily because he was almost deaf. P. happened to love his wife.

People will still recall that last heat wave. In Rome

alone over eight hundred people died of sunstroke. The streets were deserted day and night. Even the dogs kept in the shade, and many people believed that the end of the world was at hand. P. didn't believe that. He was quite interested in religious questions, but such exaggerated views struck him as foolish. The end of the world, when it did come, would be very different; or so he thought.

On one of those days Claudia, his wife, came into his study for some reason or other. P. didn't notice her come in. He happened to be reading Horace, and when he first became aware that his wife was standing behind him he was startled. He had received a sudden shock, and for a moment he was so startled that he snapped at her angrily. It wasn't his fault that he was a little deaf, he said, but at least she might show him some consideration in consequence.

"There was a time when you didn't snap my head off like that," she said reproachfully.

"Yes, yes. I know: the good old days. Everything was better then, wasn't it? I was in power and office, for example. I was in a position to do this and that for you then, I know. And now my career's ruined; I know that, and I don't need you to tell me."

"Please don't talk like that."

"I'll talk as I please and what I please. Or maybe that doesn't suit you? You've only got to say so, you know. I shall understand. I know that I'm deaf, and that my friends avoid me. I shouldn't be all that astonished if you left me in the lurch too."

At that Claudia rose and was about to leave the room.

"So, you're going. Very well."

She stopped, and said something. But he didn't understand it.

"Perhaps it's a good thing, after all, that I'm deaf," he said. "In consequence I couldn't hear what you just said. It was some sort of a reproach, of course?"

Claudia said nothing, and P. looked down at his hands and wondered what to do. If he had just said "Claudia"; nothing else—everything would have been all right. But he didn't; he said nothing. He realized that he loved his wife. How would he ever manage to get on without her? And sitting there he thought: 'I'll get up and go to her. I'll take her hand and say: "Let's make it up." I'll wait just a moment and then I'll go. I wonder what she's so angry about? I haven't really done anything. But I must say something or other now. Someone's got to make the first advance. But why me? Why does it always have to be me? She could make it up too for once, couldn't she? But no, she wouldn't dream of doing that. I've always got to be the first.'

P. looked up at her. She stood there turned away from him, but she didn't move. The heat was almost intolerable. P. looked at his hands again. 'She can stand that sort of thing a long time,' he thought. 'I know that. But I could say now: "Come on, Claudia; let's make it up." Yes, I could say that now.' But instead he said:

"Are you going to stand there like that much longer?"

"If it disturbs you I'll go," Claudia answered.

"Just as you like. Please yourself in fact. I'll tell you one thing though: if you go now then I've had enough. My life isn't all that valuable to me any more, I can tell you. I shouldn't find it difficult to put an end to it. But go by all means if you want to."

"Don't get so upset. I'm not feeling very well. Please let me go now."

And she left the room.

X

I DON'T know whether it's much use. I'm to write down my ideas, my memories, my impressions of Judea, the country and the people—something or other. What were the ostensible reasons for my removal? Why did I necessarily fail? What would I do to-day when faced with the same situation? Would I act differently? More discreetly perhaps? I'm a bit assertive of course, but that lies in my nature; it hasn't been acquired. I can't stand titles. To be called "Your Excellency" just because I was Governor never pleased me. I suspected that people were making fun of me. And it's the same the other way round. I can't bring myself to say "Venerable High Priest". I just say "Caiaphas, listen!", or "Caiaphas, come here, will you?" And they don't like that, of course; they want to be addressed by their titles.

People are used to very different masters, though in reality money, fame and popularity are very doubtful attributes for anyone with pretensions to be a gentleman. But the sad thing nowadays is that the world falls for such people. If a man has two hundred slaves, he is one slave more a gentleman than the man who has only a hundred and ninety-nine. Which means that I don't come into the running at all. Eleazar is a slave with the outlook of a gentleman, but you can't turn that sort of thing into money, and therefore it has no value.

Talking of Eleazar, I notice that he's taken to leaving the house lately, particularly after dark. I wonder what he's up to. Where does he go? And why doesn't he tell me anything about it? Or perhaps I'm just the "master" in his eyes; someone to be handled with care? But seeing that he doesn't tell me what he's up to I could ask him, of course. But what good would that do? If I have to ask him first, it means that he doesn't really want to tell me; and in that case he'll lie if I do ask him; and I don't like being lied to.

My headaches have started going down the side of my head to my right ear now. It's very odd to feel pain in an ear that's otherwise deaf and lifeless. Of course, I could go to a doctor. But who wants to have Pilate as a patient nowadays? That's the way it is with a man who has fallen into disfavour. If he gets headaches and goes to a doctor about it, the doctor thinks: 'If I treat him although he's in disfavour with the Emperor that won't do me any good.' And what will he do then? Why, he'll try to fob me off as quickly as possible.

So what should I do?

There isn't anything I can do.

XI

WHEN she had gone out of the room P. sat there and felt at a loss. Then he got up and walked up and down; telling himself that the whole business wasn't all that

43

important. All the same, he found it obsessing him more and more.

'She doesn't love me any more', he thought. 'She scolds me, marches out of the room, and leaves me on my own. I'm deaf, people show me the cold shoulder, and there's no one who cares about me any more. What's going to happen now? I'd make an end of it if I had courage enough, but I haven't. At least, I don't suppose I have. Am I too big a coward to say to myself: "There's no sense in going on. Surely you can see that?"'

His wife was sleeping. He didn't look at her, but went over to the window and leaned out. The heat was almost intolerable.

'What ought I to do?' he thought. 'If I throw myself out of the window now she'll be sorry. She'll weep, and tell herself she was fond of me. She'll kiss my hands and see them growing whiter and colder. She'll take my head against her breasts and stroke my hair . . . Perhaps one ought to do something like that.

'It would be blackmail though. And brutal. I can't control my thoughts. They do as they please. And what now?'

"I believe I could commit suicide and you wouldn't bother much," he said aloud.

He heard no reply to his remark. Had she really nothing to say? Or had she said something he hadn't heard? He leant out of the window and looked down into the street. There was a cat in the street but he took no notice of it. What did cats matter to him? He had other troubles. He was annoyed that his wife should be asleep. He wouldn't have been able to sleep in the circumstances. But everyone had to settle that sort of thing for himself.

Then he went to bed.
Long after midnight he was still awake.
His wife was dead.

XII

THE next morning Stephanio came. He was the first
visitor after Claudia's death. Forty-six days—I've marked
them off the calendar one by one—I've been alone now.
I was surprised at his visit. I clearly remembered our first
meeting. I was fifteen or sixteen at the time. I didn't feel
inclined to remind him of it. Incidentally, I hear better
within my own four walls.

I had squabbled with my father at the time and left
the house. I was always one for being alone, and usually,
when I couldn't stand it at home any more, I would walk
to the banks of the Tiber. Even in those days there was
a very mixed public in the parks, including many doubtful
characters; though it wasn't so bad then as it is now. But
the rumour-mongers went about their evil business even
then. I was always inclined to prefer my own company
to other people's, and I could quite easily find my
favourite sandy bank even to-day. That is, if it still exists.
I wonder. Perhaps one day I'll go and see.

I was sitting on the sandy bank looking into the water,
idly letting the dry sand run through my fingers, and
thinking just as idly. Was my father my real father? If
he were why was I so totally different from him? What
was to become of me? I had no idea. I might have become

a teacher, but I should never have been able to get my father to agree to that.

And then I felt that someone was watching me. A young fellow came towards me over the meadow. Stephanio is about my own age; perhaps a year or two younger even. He was very cheerful then, laughing and even whistling a popular tune, tearing clumps of grass out of the earth and throwing them into the air and clapping his hands. He looked on top of the world. Stephanio was a gay, carefree sort of lad, quite the opposite of me. He sat down on the bank, but pretended that he hadn't seen me, pulled out a blade of grass and began to chew it, at the same time squinting over to where I was sitting. I knew that he was going to tease me, and so I said nothing and wondered how I could make my escape. Right up to my years in the army I firmly believed that there were certain secret and mysterious powers in the world: you only had to think about a thing hard enough, for example, and it came to pass. So I closed my eyes and wished firmly that Stephanio should be turned there and then into a goat, a fish or a dog. All you've got to do is to concentrate sufficiently on it, I told myself, and when you open your eyes again Stephanio will be, say, a wretched little mongrel, which you can drive away. But when I opened my eyes and looked in Stephanio's direction, there he was still, grinning at me. My secret powers weren't much good apparently. I was disappointed, and I splashed in the water with my foot and looked at the waves. Let him start talking if he wants to, I thought. But he took his time.

In the end he asked me if I wasn't speaking to him. Was I annoyed with him about something? I don't remember any more just what he did say, although in such things which lie back many years my memory is usually very good indeed. In the small things of everyday life it is less reliable now. Eleazar has to remind me of something or other every day. But as soon as any question arises about even the smallest episode of our days in Judea my memory is almost always better than his. I could make a very detailed sketch of my garden in Caesarea even now, and I don't think there would be any mistakes. I can remember every plant and bush. But that's all over now.

Stephanio is much older, of course. We all are. He still talks a lot, but only about himself and the theatre. Apart from that he's inclined to backbite. He doesn't think much of the modern theatre. The "great actors" have died out, he says. He certainly felt himself entitled to call himself one of them, the last of the line perhaps. The younger generation was more interested in the circus than the arts. Actors had suffered a good deal on that account. They hadn't always, I must remember, thought of nothing but money and fame. And then he told me about one actor he knew who had brought the ashes of his beloved brother on to the stage in an urn in order to create the doleful atmosphere he needed for his part.

But Stephanio was glad he wasn't on the stage any more, or so he assured me. I didn't believe him though. In fact I was quite certain that he was being dishonest and it struck me as odd that even a good actor couldn't lie convincingly. I tried repeatedly to turn the conversation to some other subject, but in vain. He isn't interested in anything else. One or two remarks he did make about politics and literature were terribly pedestrian; worse even than that; they sounded as though he had read them somewhere or other and didn't know quite what

47

to make of them, but thought they sounded all right.

After he had busily torn everyone else to pieces, he began to flatter me to the top of his bent. In his view I was a martyr to duty, he said. I ought to try for an interview with the Emperor, or see what Cassius could do for me, in order to get back into favour again. The talents of a man like me ought not to be wasted; that was to the detriment of Rome and the world. He was speaking really seriously, he assured me.

Fiddlesticks!

Before he left he borrowed money from me. I'm annoyed that I gave him any now.

XIII

CLAUDIA always found it very difficult to give her hand to anyone who was not really amiably inclined towards her. She always said that it positively hurt her, and she would shudder. I never had such sensitive feelings. I'm much too inclined to let myself be deceived by other people. At first I was even silly enough to feel flattered by Stephanio's gross compliments. And yet I have very good reason to be cautious and mistrustful. All the same, I can't. Now the Town Prefect of Jerusalem, a man in the middle years who died shortly after my recall—there was a rumour that he had been poisoned; it was all very mysterious. . . . Now what was his name again?

I have cudgelled my brains to remember it. And yet I was closely connected with the fellow for over ten years;

I talked to him frequently, I wrote to him often—and now I can't even remember his name. I went through all the letters of the alphabet one after the other, but although his name was on the tip of my tongue I just couldn't get it. Never mind, it doesn't matter. . . . Well, anyway, what I was going to say was I was never careful enough where he was concerned either. He was too obsequious, too zealous, and always so anxious to do me a favour at a moment's notice. Such people should be treated with suspicion. Claudia was always warning me against him. She said he was "insincere". He probably was, but I had no proof. Everything about him was correct: his work, the way he dressed. And he never drank too much either. . . .

Ah! I've got it! Burrus was his name. Town Prefect Burrus. Sometimes I think he had a finger in the pie when I was recalled, but there again, I've no proof. Incidentally, I've just come across one of his reports amongst my papers:[1]

"Precautionary measures were taken in Jerusalem in connection with the Feast of the Passover, particularly on account of the presence of many pilgrims not only from Judea but from many other provinces of the Roman Empire. The patrols were strengthened in all parts of the town, and special commandos were stationed at particularly dangerous points.

"The celebrations went off on the whole more peacefully than at Easter. A few pickpockets were caught, a few brawls were broken up, and a number of money-changers were fined.

"But to-day at about three o'clock in the morning something very strange and inexplicable took place in the Upper Town near the aqueduct which bears your name. Three patrols of four men each happened to be in the neighbourhood and

[1] The original was listed by me as VIIc-III-Ba., and is appended. L.P.B.

49

they met in front of a large house in which a number of followers of the man Christ you had crucified six weeks ago were gathered. These people have been under special supervision since then of course, but they have given us no cause to take any action against them. All you could hear from the house was praying and singing day and night.

"Now all our men report unanimously that at about three o'clock in the morning there was a sudden rushing sound around the house as though a great storm had sprung up. They all saw a glaring light, and a number of what looked like flashes of lightning. This bright light filled the whole house, which did not, however, catch fire. The rushing sound and the brilliance both lasted for some time, and the soldiers were able to observe the phenomena clearly.

"The great noise awakened the neighbours and the pilgrims staying in the quarter and soon masses of people were flocking together to watch the unusual scene. Before long several thousand people were gathered, and Decurio asked for the reinforcement of the patrols. I immediately sent him all the men I could spare from other parts of the town.

"Suddenly the door of the house opened and eleven men came out. At their head was a man named Cephas, a fellow who had been seen around a good deal with the man Jesus. Behind them were other people, including women. This man Cephas now turned to the assembled people and addressed them in a loud voice. This preliminary report is not the place to record all he said, but according to the unanimous version of all our men he announced that Jesus of Nazareth who had been crucified had since arisen from the dead. In fact I was there to hear his last words myself. They were: 'Repent, and be baptized everyone of you in the name of Jesus Christ for the remission of sins. Save yourself from this accursed generation.'

"Now the really odd thing, Your Excellency, is that this man Cephas spoke in Galilean dialect, and yet what he said was understood in their own languages by all who heard him. For example, I heard what he said in Latin, my soldiers heard him in Greek, Gallic, Syrian, and so on, according to their mother tongues. Apart from a very few who regarded this

Cephas as drunk most people were deeply impressed by what they had seen and heard; so much so that many of them—perhaps three thousand—did let themselves be baptized. And amongst them were some of our own men, including Captain Longinus. I could not see that his behaviour conflicted in any way with Army Regulations, and therefore I did not interfere.

"That in short, Your Excellency, is a summary of the strange happening. In the meantime I shall, of course, have the closest investigation made and set down in writing. The matter strikes me as so important as to suggest that your own presence in Jerusalem would be desirable. When people get carried away like this there is no knowing what they may do.

"(Sig.) Burrus
"Town Prefect

"Post scriptum: I send this urgent
report closed and sealed, and request
an acknowledgement of receipt."

What can a man make of muddle-headed babbling like that? And this stupid "Your Excellency" here and "Your Excellency" there; and the totally unnecessary reference to the fact that the aqueduct bears my name (that is to say, it did bear my name; it won't any more!) —what place should such things have in an objective official report? A few hysterical Jews suffer from religious hallucinations. What does the man expect me to do about it? Even if one or two of my own men do catch it too? What did he think he was Town Prefect for anyway? He knew as well as I did that the Jews suffered from religious mania and discovered a new Messiah every other week. So why all this obsequious fuss and bother? Was it in order to impress me and make me realize what a zealous and responsible subordinate I had? That was a trifle too naïve of him, since I knew him to be a man incapable of separating the essential from the inessential —from the fleas in the cracks in the wall, for example. But

he was only doing his duty I suppose. Responsibility? I
don't think he felt any, or if he did he was too scared to
take it and wanted to pass it on to me. But perhaps the
thing isn't as simple as that?

XIV

ANOTHER visit from Stephanio. Now what's he up to?
His pretext was that he thought I ought to know about a
new rumour he had heard. By chance he happened to be
passing the Eastern Gate it appeared—I know such
"chances"! In a side street close to the house of Plinius
he noticed a group of people. "As though casually" he
joined them. A well-known rumour-monger—he did
mention the fellow's name, but I've already forgotten it
—was talking about me. This man is very popular by all
accounts, but I don't know much about such matters.

According to Stephanio the fellow said that whilst I was
Governor of Judea I had done a lot of harm. I was too
feeble and too brutal by turns; and my methods of
administering justice had offended both Roman citizens
and Jews alike. According to Stephanio the fellow then
said that it was "high time" the Emperor called me to
account for my wrongdoings. Now how much of all
this is of any importance to-day? Haven't people got
anything better to do than rummage around in the past?
And who's interested, and why?

The trick of this man and his like is to spread half-
truths. They don't positively lie. They can prove that if

you challenge them. They quote facts. From someone or other behind the scenes they know all sorts of trivial facts, such as what a man eats or drinks, and his general habits. And if they find out that now and again he has drunk too much and perhaps said an incautious word, they've got him. Of course, the people they slander can take them to court, but as a writ against a real lie is almost unfair so a writ against the half-truth is almost hopeless. It's not a question of an easy conscience so much as a long arm; and they usually have that.

Whoever has power abuses it; that's a fact, and everything else is nonsense.

Apparently this rumour-monger had found out something about my talks with Barabbas—"Relations with a rebel". "Conversations of a very friendly nature", to quote the man's words, who then demanded to know whether I could deny it, and answered the question himself by saying that I couldn't. According to him I also couldn't deny that I had not only spared this criminal, an enemy of Rome, but had actually protected him.

Of course you can't deny that sort of thing. From what muddy sources does such a fellow obtain his information, and why aren't those punished from whom he obtains it? How did this man even know of the existence of Barabbas; not to speak of my relationship to him? I'm quite sure that if you asked him to write it down you'd find he couldn't write. But he pronounces it confidently in public and thus creates the impression of being very well informed. People therefore believe him; what he says is true; and therefore Pilate is a scoundrel. Such men are very cunning, and, given the opportunity, they may become very dangerous one day.

According to Stephanio the fellow said that I was an

incompetent Governor, and that if historians ever mentioned my name it would be only to condemn me. In which, I'm afraid, the fellow does me too much honour. They're not likely to mention me one way or the other.

He also said that during my term of office the situation in Judea was catastrophic, worse than at any other time. I hadn't been clever enough to work sensibly with the Sanhedrim or the political parties, or energetic enough to deal with the rebels. In consequence my successor had found himself faced with appalling and quite unnecessary difficulties. At that, I had to laugh, and it struck me that the best cure for that chap would be a course of negotiations with the Sanhedrim. On the other hand, you never know; they might have got on famously together.

And finally, the man was anxious to persuade his hearers that the best thing to do would be to put me out of harm's way without more ado.

Well, that's a nice state of affairs, I must say! Open agitation against a man's life on the public streets! For some time I sat and thought the matter over, wondering whether I ought to do something about it. But what purpose would that serve. Nowadays the courts are more corrupt than ever, and they would be against me from the start. But who could have paid this fellow to talk like that? Cassius perhaps? Or my successor in Judea? Incidentally, I'm not surprised that the business with my predecessor Pontius Aquilus has been brought up again. Why shouldn't they use a man who took an active part in Caesar's assassination against his grandsons? That's the sort of people they are; any stick's good enough to beat a mangy dog with. The great thing is that they can make something out of it.

It makes me sick.

Naturally, Stephanio told me all this in the greatest confidence, and "only in my own interests", of course. He needn't have mentioned the confidential part of it; I know perfectly well that if it suited him he would deny every word he had said. "What, m'lud! 'I' said that! But m'lud, you know me too well . . ." I know him too well too.

You are alone in death. Perhaps it's a good thing that I'm getting deafer every day.

And yet Stephanio's a bit of a puzzle to me. Young girls still regard him as "a handsome man". But he never wanted to have anything much to do with *them*—at least, he didn't when he was young. He has good manners, he speaks in a theatrical voice, he gives himself out as well-educated and he preens himself on his good nature. But he never has any opinions of his own. For example, you'll hear him talking of Horace as naturally as about the weather, and yet I'm perfectly convinced that he doesn't understand a line. He talks to people as his belly guides him; he thinks far too much of himself; and, in particular, he seems to think he's found a willing victim for his babble. It doesn't disturb him that I'm deaf. With astonishing and dangerous frankness he tells me everything he thinks, or pretends to think, and I can't make out what he's after. Of course, he knows that although I've got one leg in the grave, I still have to reckon with chicanery. For example, the Emperor might take the rumour-monger more seriously than I do. What then? He might stop my pension, or even banish me altogether.

But people don't bother a great deal about the individual nowadays. No one crucifies us, no one stones us, and no one flogs us half dead before the execution—in any case, a crucifixion isn't half as bad as old women who

55

dote on their lap dogs imagine. But in any case, we are much more humane these days. We allow an old servant of the State, who once enjoyed fame and honour, and even rose to the eminence of Governor, to go to the dogs quietly and most humanely; but very certainly for all that. If a man is torn to pieces in public by the Emperor's lions—in the circus to the great enjoyment of all present, or if he is stoned by the Emperor's soldiers, or crucified, then at least he has the chance of remaining someone; if only a decent sort of fellow; though he might also be a martyr to something or other. But what am I? A state pensioner, a deaf old good-for-nothing, a shabby old ex-Governor. And not, all in all, a very admirable character.

In the so-called "upper classes" everyone is a bit of a poseur nowadays. Everyone is playing some role or other: Emperor, Senator, estate agent, Governor, medicine man, benefactor. But whatever it is, they act. And in reality they're quite different from whatever it is they pretend to be. For example, they are "considerate" towards their wives, but they get their own way all the same; they are "aristocratic", but they haven't the faintest notion of nobility. They boast: "Without servants I could live just as well as I do now." But in reality they don't even know how to fold their own togas! They say there's nothing they desire more than to see a world without hatred, without enmity and without war; but try to take away even a single one of their four hundred slaves and they'll bash you on the head, smash your face in, and nail you to the cross.

As far as I'm concerned there's only one possible thing, and that is to remain Pilate. But why?

Perhaps I've become a moralist. Morality, of course,

not as a mere label. I don't care how anyone lives. I have
no objection to seducers, villains, rumour-mongers and
posturing actors. They've all as much right to exist as I
have. But I do object when an actor who is playing the
part of Pan imagines he really is Pan. And I do object
when a rumour-monger thinks himself a personality just
because the mob listens to him open-mouthed. And I
protest when an estate agent declares that he furthers the
public welfare. He does nothing of the sort; he merely
profits by it.

May one say that out loud nowadays?

No doubt about it, I'm cowardly too. I take the
Emperor's money though I disagree with his policy and
abominate his taste, and although I do nothing whatever
for it, I console myself with the truthful circumstance
that he does even less himself, and with the thought that
I pocket his money with an ironical smile and not with the
stupid feeling that I have honestly earned it. If I ever did
anything good then it was against the Empire. All I ever
did for the Empire was to hang or crucify a few poor
wretches. And I'm living on that still. If I had crucified a
few more I should have a few more denarii to-day. It's
as simple as that. But denarii are not mere money, they
are recognition, slaves, friends, invitations, honour. Make
what you can of that!

As a matter of fact I always thought a good deal
before imposing a death sentence. But nowadays people
seem to suppose that all the chief of an occupation authority does is to live in luxury, bathe in the sea when it
suits him, crucify a few people now and again, drink a
lot of wine in the evening and sleep it off the following
morning until midday.

No one bothers about the dead. They are dead and we

are still alive. What for? A nice funeral perhaps? And what about me?

I'm bored. I feel superfluous. I write. I think. But what for? We all have our funny little ways. The spirit of the age is all in favour of noise and to-do, and, of course, money; and I can't get very enthusiastic about any of it. The spirit of the age believes in Rome and world rule, but I get pains in my joints when there's going to be rain. The world worships tittle-tattle, sensations, tame lions, brothels, an authoritarian Emperor, drinking orgies and profitable rackets.

My teacher Fabricius said: "Everyone believes what he wants to believe." The Greeks had other gods because they wanted other gods. Mem.: read Plato's "Ring of Gyges". We don't understand them because we can't establish any real relationship with history. For example, your modern Rome has only the vaguest idea about Pan. It takes quite a well-educated Roman to know that Pan was a Greek god who lived in a cave, who loved the heat of the day and helped to win the battle of Marathon.

A real relationship?

The good Roman citizen has other gods. With scent from Alexandria dabbed behind his ears, and wearing a newly-tailored toga round his middle he reads verses of Homer. And he really believes that he understands something of what he reads. In fact he even says "his" Homer. That's much as though the people who will live, say, five hundred years after us and can perhaps fly through the air, will imagine they know just what Rome looked like in our day. What sort of a "relationship" can such people have to us—from the air, five hundred years later, and with quite different eyes?

They could for example, sum me up as deaf, lazy

brutal and hostile to the State. And that's just about the opposite of what I really am—apart from the deafness.

It's dangerous that the idiocies of to-day are getting more and more idiotic. When I was young we were, of course, lively and cheerful, and we made jokes; and now and again some of them weren't in the best taste. But youth to-day has no respect for anything. They make a great deal of noise, they bawl in the streets at night, and they attack old and helpless people; all because they're bored and don't know what to do with themselves. They've got no aim in life. Rome is Rome, and what had to be done for Rome has already been done. Eleazar was telling me the other day about a young fellow who opened an office for commercial marriage-broking! Only a little while ago, Lepida, a granddaughter of the Emperor if you please, committed suicide in order to avoid conviction (adultery with a slave). The trend to abnormality is frightening. Nowadays deformed people are put on show for people to gaze at their deformities. Eleazar was telling me that he had seen a boy who weighed only seventeen pounds, wasn't two feet tall, and yet had a stentorian voice. And according to the journals, the Emperor has received the following presents from India: a man without arms, three vipers, a snake over twenty feet long, a river turtle six feet across, and a partridge which is bigger than a vulture.

Where will such perverse lusts lead to?

Legal training is declining every day. My father was a cunning and not particularly scrupulous advocate even in his day, but he was a good lawyer. Nowadays you don't have to know anything about law at all, and the profession is open to anyone from Senator to manumitted slave. And as oratory and cunning count for everything, and morality and law for practically nothing, the biggest rogues are now becoming advocates. Naturally they are only interested in making money, and nothing is too unscrupulous to be beneath them. They will accept everything: money, wine, hams, precious stones, purple cloaks, just everything. Statues grow up like mushrooms in front of their houses, and every time they win a case they put a laurel wreath over their doors. They'll do anything for publicity. Their profession brings them neither titles nor reputation, so at least they want money. Before they address the court they behave like actors; they drink glass after glass of water to show how indignant and excited they are, then they declaim a lot of rubbish with theatrical pathos; and in order that everyone shall notice how clever and educated they are they throw in a few comments on the Punic Wars or on Sulla's verse. It's all outward show, and beforehand they take good care to hire a suitable claque to cheer them; and promise the judge a good part of their fees if he decides in their favour. In fact only the other day an advocate was convicted for having accepted payment from the other side to ruin his own client's chances. Naturally, you can't keep that sort of thing from people for long, and the result is they're beginning to refer to advocacy only in contemptuous terms.

And to think that Rome was once a State based on law! Not that our present-day advocates mind that—so long as the money keeps rolling in.

XV

WE were too victorious. And we got into the habit of ignoring the feelings of a defeated people and the interests of their country. They lost the war, we think, so they've no right to say anything. They've just got to do as the victor tells them.

I wonder.

And as for the occupation itself, people here think that the Governor of a subjugated province is just a fortunate man who lives in a beautiful villa with a lovely garden, and has soldiers to guard him, and do his bidding, and hold the population down. What else should he have to do?

As against such facile impressions I have to record that the Palestinian Jews managed to obtain my recall, and that, far from being their master, I, the Governor of Judea and representative of the Emperor, was their victim.

I am not interested in defending myself. The babble of the rumour-mongers and of those people who are always so anxious to spread the very latest scandal is not very pleasant, of course, but at least I can't help feeling that to be its subject does me honour. To be praised by them is never a recommendation. No, as far as I am concerned what I am really interested in in these jottings is a problem which has occupied me for a good few years of my life. Perhaps you could formulate the first question as follows:

What means, methods and laws are best calculated to

safeguard the rights of the occupying power and at the same time to allow the defeated a real measure of at least relative independence? That I approach this problem from a practical angle, and with the specific example of Judea in mind, goes without saying.[1]

The argument that the victor is in the right just because he is the victor is not acceptable to the vanquished. They regard themselves as an oppressed people, and they claim that oppression can never be right. They are both proud and mistrustful at the same time. The proud ones will refuse a gift from the Governor, whilst the distrustful will not shake hands with an ordinary soldier for fear of being bewitched. If the occupation Governor is strict the people will hate him, whilst if he is humane they will regard him as weak and incompetent. If he tries to be just without respect to persons, he will not get far either, because people have different ideas of justice and injustice.

An example of this: one of the first problems I was faced with in Judea was to arrive at some sort of working compromise with the Messiah mania of the Jews. They were firmly convinced, if not for one reason then for another, that a "Messiah" would come and liberate them and bring them the victory over Rome. And anyone, soothsayer, priest, astrologer, or simple charlatan, who exploited this belief was sure of a hearing. It is difficult for an occupying power to keep such people under control.

Now those feelings of religious mania were steadily intensifying. During the final years of my governorship

[1] How dull and clumsy language becomes when you are using it not for yourself but for a few blockheads to whom you wish to make your own attitude clear! But why does a man bother in the first place? P.P.

there was a new "Messiah" practically once a week. Some people believed in him, others didn't; with the result that before long the squabbling developed into rioting, the people became restive, and numerous scoundrels exploited the credulity of the mob either for political or commercial motives. The Jews expected that this "Messiah" would liberate them from Roman bondage, annihilate the "heathen", abolish our poll tax, bring "not peace but a sword", and make the Jews the people of all peoples. The Messiah himself would be, they believed, "the adopted son of the Jewish God"; and in a document we confiscated was the prophecy: "And thou, O Israel, shall be blest, and tread on the neck and wings of the Roman Eagle."

Here, of course, such things sound fantastic and ridiculous, and I have often been asked why I tolerated the whole business. Why didn't I take stern measures? Why didn't I root out the people responsible?

But as I have always pointed out, my duty was to maintain law and order. There was quite enough killing and murder as it was. And further, our military strength there was quite inadequate for real trouble, and we should not have been able to deal with a general rising of the population if it had come. It was therefore a counsel of prudence, and a matter of loyalty to the Emperor and to Rome, to try as far as possible to prevent all these squabbles and disputes from developing into open rebellion. And for this reason it seemed wise to me not to interfere with the institution of Jewish justice more than was absolutely necessary. As far as possible let them try each other without interference from us. This had the great advantage of making me the final arbiter, their court of appeal, a largely neutral resort, and allowing me to hold myself aloof from their disputes. I think I can really say that this policy was successful.

In fact, only once throughout the whole years of my governorship did the Jews succeed in dragging one of those fellows who claimed to be the Messiah before me. And that particular fellow wasn't of much importance. He was a feeble type, yielding in character and poor in physique, with a weak chest. He was the son of an odd-job carpenter and he was quite certainly not an enemy of the State. However, I'm wandering from the point, and in any case, the digression isn't likely to be of any general interest.

Now Barabbas is a typical example of the problem I am discussing—mem.: set down my conversation with him; title: "On Superstition."

He started off as an enemy of the Roman Empire, as a rebel, as a "Hero of the People". But, like all of us, he became older, and began to put on girth, and, after that he lived on the laurels of the past. Finally, as frequently happens with such people, he fell victim to religious mania. He firmly believed in visions, ghosts and miracles. His eyes would become glazed, he would lose all sense of reality, and he would rave about "his" Messiah as one might about some unapproachable beloved wor-shipped only from afar. And when I deigned to occupy myself with his superstitious follies, and took the trouble to drive him into a corner with logical arguments he always had a few evasive phrases ready, such as "Ah, but he was the son of God!", or, quite conclusively from his point of view, "He died for me".

Of course, in Rome people laugh about such things and shrug their shoulders. How could you have taken such things seriously! But for the chief of the occupation power such things *are* serious. He has to deal with the most incredible stupidities, and he can't dismiss them on that account. Incidentally, precisely those people who say I ought never to have listened to Barabbas in the first place are those who reproach me in the next breath for what they call my greatest mistake—namely, not keeping my ear to the ground and finding out what the mob was thinking. They think they understand everything much better. I'd like to ask them what they do understand. The Emperor is . . .[1]

XVI

I WAS in town for the second time since Claudia's death. I can't yet grasp the fact that she is dead, and I find myself thinking: 'I hope she hasn't caught cold!'; 'I wonder what she really thinks of Stephanio'; 'Didn't she say I was to bring back something or other?'; 'I'll have to hurry up or I'll be late for dinner.' But then I remember that I shan't be too late any more. 'She is dead,' I think, and I stop—because I can think better when I'm standing still —close my eyes, and wait a moment or two. . . . Then I begin to notice that people are staring at me and obviously wondering what's the matter with me.

There's nothing the matter with me of course. Some-one passes, greets me, and is about to give me his hand. I don't know him do I? Or do I? I don't know, and so

[1] The deleted words have been rendered illegible by me out of proper respect for the Emperor. L.P.B.

he goes on. I have an idea that he turns round and looks back at me. Perhaps he thinks I'm a trifle strange, or even a little unhinged. And then—quite suddenly—there's that stabbing pain between my forehead and the crown of my head. It always starts in the same place. At first it's little more than a tremor, quite gentle, but returning at regular intervals. Then it establishes itself and stabs in all directions: in the forehead, in the scalp, behind the ears and just under the eyes. And then it makes the first stab into the brain. That's what I always wait for. Once it's in the brain then the worst is over. It's in the brain, of course, stabbing, throbbing, quivering—but at least it doesn't surprise me any more. There it is, and there's nothing I can do about it. The worst part is the preliminary, the starting up, the tentative stabs.

I really don't know my way around in the town any more. Nowadays Rome has more public parks than poor people, more palaces than princes to live in them. Before long there'll be only the palaces left; and by that time the poor will be rich and the rich poor—and then the whole business will start again from the beginning. A man who has been able to live even a few years of his life in ordered circumstances is lucky.

That's naturally no consolation; but what is consolation anyway? When someone, referring to the death of my wife, says: "Don't let it upset you"?

I wanted to go down to the banks of the Tiber and look at the water. An odd idea, but when such odd ideas crop up there's no reason why I shouldn't follow them. Of course, I didn't carry out my intention—when do I ever? I met the house tutor of Cassius; my headache started up on the way; I saw a cat; stopped and wondered whether to take it along with me. 'But perhaps she won't want to come!' I thought. 'Perhaps she'll spit at me if I try to pick her up. Perhaps she'll run away, and the people in the street will laugh at me for an old fool. And, in any case, perhaps her owners have turned her out because she's mangy or something. And why do I want to take her with me anyway? What should I do with a cat? I wonder who feeds her? Why do I get such ideas? Because Claudia's dead? Because the cat looks half-starved? Human beings often look half-starved, and no one bothers much about that. So why should I bother about the cat?'

That constant why, why, why, always gives me a headache. If I were a doctor and had me for a patient I'd soon put a stop to that profitless questioning.

Very well, I wanted to go down to the Tiber, but on the way I came to the market place where they display freaks, and there I saw a human being wallowing in his own filth. He couldn't stand or walk, or speak a sensible word, and although he had the face of a forty-year-old he wasn't bigger than a two-year-old child. He was unshaven, had an unkempt beard, a great mop of hair and no teeth. He paid no attention to the sightseers, but just sat there swaying backwards and forwards and sucking his crippled toes. Then I saw a woman without legs, and she was naked. The skin of the stumps was flabby, and light red in colour, and it wobbled. The woman grinned at me. She was obviously mad, but suddenly it occurred to me that she probably regarded me as mad. 'And who's to say which of us is right?' I thought. A man with a great hunch on his back was throwing himself backwards on to it until it seemed as though the hunch must burst. He grinned at me too, and seemed to guess my thoughts. Laughing and making animal-like

67

noises he begged for money, and I gave him a little.

After that I went home. I had forgotten the Tiber and that I wanted to look at its waters again.

If I had a hunch on my back I shouldn't try to earn money that way. I'd live against my hunch, I think. That's easily said, of course. When you live at all you live against something. And if you live—as I do—against an Emperor, against rumour-mongers, against deaf ears, and against the vulgar mob in general, why shouldn't you also live against a hunch on your back?

Eleazar is out of the house again. That's happening a lot lately. I wonder where he is and what he's doing? And why? Some more of those whys, you see! But you just live, think, read, write, eat, sleep, have headaches; and so on and so on.

XVII

STEPHANIO still has a good appearance. He speaks without accent or dialect in a fine, well-modulated voice. But he doesn't know what he's saying. When I first saw him on the stage he was still young and comparatively unknown, and I liked him. I remember once he was hauled before the courts for being disorderly in the streets at night, and my father defended him. Stephanio lies as everyone lies nowadays. (Must lie? Wants to lie? Can only lie?) But he lies differently. He lies like an actor. When he says "My dear Pilate," you'd think he were on the stage declaiming. But here and now it sounds hollow. And he's vain, of course. His vanity consists in assuring you again and again that he's not vain. He will wait for hours before my house until he sees me coming home from town, and then he'll hide himself, and a few minutes later he'll come in and say: "I just happened to be passing." Of course, he's quite convinced that all the girls in Rome look after him in the street, but it's only the other sort he's really interested in, and as soon as he spots a homosexual he minces and becomes self-conscious. But the homosexual probably hasn't even noticed him, being too busy thinking about his income-tax return. All his colleagues are "amiable", "nice", or even "charming". But they're never actors. "Did you notice how badly A. did that?" he will ask. Or "Don't you think B. hams dreadfully?"

But he doesn't give you a chance to say what you think anyway. He just takes it for granted that you agree with him, and goes on: "Yes, that's what I always think too. I'm completely in agreement with you." But whether it's a youth, a man, a woman, or a comedian, only Stephanio can play the role properly.

He is always outwardly in agreement with everybody. He would never say "You're wrong," or even "I can't say." He will agree with everything you say. He will join with you, or with anyone else, in abusing anyone at all, but he is never disagreeable to the person he happens to be speaking to at the moment. If I were to say that the Emperor is an idiot, he would reply that there was something to be said for that point of view; and then if, a little later, I were to say that the Emperor is a highly intelligent man, he would reply at once: "Oh, yes, of course! I've always thought so."

He's always playing a role, the same one—himself.

He can't just walk into a room casually like anyone else; he has to "make an entrance". If he got very drunk and ended up by sleeping it off in the gutter, his first words when he woke up would be: "Now how did I play that?"

XVIII

PERHAPS my judgement on Stephanio is unjust. After all, other people might think that way about me. Perhaps someone somewhere makes a note in his diary: "Pilate is an upright man." Then pauses and thinks: 'But is he? No, he isn't because he hasn't courage enough to tell the Emperor what he really thinks. He is weak, unstable, and much too dependent on his wife. And he's a liar too. He'll tell you now that he loved his wife, but in reality he plagued her. He shouted at her, deceived her and pestered her with his jealousy. He's a drinker too, though he tries to keep it quiet. He'd like to have us believe that he's an intelligent, cultured and well-read man, and that he was an enlightened Governor. But he's really no better than the rest of them.'

Well, is Pilate an upright man?

Sometimes he's too lazy even to wash himself properly. And sometimes he's too drunk to undress. He's a vain man too. He wants people to believe that he was a good and enlightened Governor, but he wasn't really. He's a weak man. In his own house he lets himself go, wipes his eye and feels sorry for himself, but in public he likes to pretend he's vigorous and determined. And he's not a just man either. He was unkind to his wife when she was alive.

That will do.

My headache is coming on again.

XIX

I HAD an invitation from Cassius, but I wasn't very pleased about it. At one time I should have turned it down because I didn't care to act against my convictions. But the situation is different to-day. Since Claudia's death I seem numbed. Why should I incur his resentment by refusing to accept his invitation? I can't afford to anyway. Nowadays he has the power I once had; and compared with the danger of a slanderous observation about me to the Emperor, it's the lesser evil to accept the invitation—however unwillingly. In any case, I'm sick and tired of playing the upright and honourable man.

Cassius takes a good deal of trouble to make himself appear even richer than he actually is. Of course, that isn't difficult when you *are* well off. There was enough food and drink there for another hundred guests. Some of them had their breath taken away at the sight of that vast spread, but not me; I have to be careful with mine; I don't know how much longer it will have to last. Of course, it wasn't that Cassius was so anxious that all his guests should have everything they wanted: he was just out to show them what he could afford when he gave a banquet. And most of his guests were properly envious, but not me; I wasn't able to do him that favour. I didn't feel envious. Let Cassius eat roast pheasant if he wants to; personally I prefer roast pork. He noticed that I wasn't very cheerful, and he looked in my direction more than once. So at the first opportunity I excused myself with my deafness. That was hypocrisy, of course, but such banquets couldn't be held at all without a little hypocrisy.

Actually I found the whole business a bit tiresome. For one thing I knew very few of the guests. The new rich change almost from hour to hour in Rome nowadays. I did exchange a few words with Fluvius and later on with Stephanio. The affair lasted until far into the night, and when I noticed that most of them were drunk I left.

A different world that. You get the impression that none of them ever does anything, but if you ask them everyone tells you that he's so busy he hardly knows whether he's standing on his head or his heels. Their days are completely occupied. There are visits first thing in the morning, followed by a business appointment, a discreet discussion, and a personal interview. After that they have to go to a poetry reading, though they really aren't interested in poetry. And finally they hurry into court, or to the Chief Magistrate, or to the Temple of Diana, to a wedding or to a sick-bed. And they spend the night eating and drinking with a false friend like Cassius. And what have they done? Nothing at all. They were just there. Not that it matters to me.

I got very little out of it all. If you're both sober and deaf such affairs don't mean much to you. The only thing I heard Cassius say was to suggest that the poor ought to be sent out of Rome because their presence spoiled the view. After which he turned directly to me and asked whether there wouldn't be room for them in Judea. Ask silly questions and you get silly answers, so I told him the place was over-populated already. Cassius took that one in and nodded wisely.

Idiot!

The evening began quietly enough. A choir of freed slaves sang, Stephanio recited Virgil and Horace, there were dance mimes, and a company of actors I didn't know staged a comedy I didn't know. Whilst we were eating there was music on the lyre and the flute, but there at least my deafness stood me in good stead and I didn't hear a note of it. Half the dishes placed before us were unknown to me, and what half the food was called and where it came from were mysteries to me. I don't bother my head much about such things anyway.

After that came the "entertaining" part of the evening. Andalusian dancers, the one more opulent than the other, sang bawdy songs accompanied by appropriate gestures. Then came a lot of smut. Two innocently-dressed children were brought on, and no matter what questions they were asked they always gave a reply which was obscene no matter how harmless the question. A story teller regaled us with intimate revelations. Then Cassius distributed money, in order that his "beloved guests" might take part in the gambling at his expense. When even the Emperor writes a book about games of chance, what do you expect. . . .[1] And what did we talk about? The weather. As Seneca says somewhere: "The foolish babble of those searching for words!" Were sea foods more digestible than land produce? Which came first, the chicken or the egg? Why Pythagoras says you mustn't eat fish. Whether

[1] A few lines in the manuscript have been made illegible at this point by their author. L.P.B.

the Jews refuse to eat pork out of respect or contempt for the pig. Who is the god of the Jews? The demoralizing effect of modern music. In which hand Diomedes wounded Venus. Do the games make the gladiators tired? At what age is a racehorse at the height of its powers? And then, of course: "Do you know how much L. had to pay for his mistress?" "Have you heard that Titus owes Lipus 700,000 sesterces?" . . . that R. has become homosexual . . . that V. indulges in bestiality? And so on.

That's the sort of thing that interests Roman society.

Stephanio wanted to have my unvarnished opinion of the Emperor, but I gave him an evasive answer. When each man distrusts his neighbour then conversation becomes either stupid or swinish. By the way, I heard that Cassius pays his driver twenty thousand sesterces. Why so much? Because the man's deaf, and that's very convenient. Perhaps I'll look for a job as a deaf driver myself. . . .

XX

I READ in M.: "You're a gentleman, Cotilus, so many people say. What is a gentleman? One who keeps his locks in fashionable order, always smells of balsam and cinnamon, hums the melodies of Alexandrine and Spanish dances, moves with the grace of a dancer, spends the whole day with women, always whispering this or that into someone's ear, writing missives, reading the missives of others, takes good care not to let his elbow come into contact with others, who knows with what girl he's in love, who goes from banquet to banquet, and knows the pedigree of every thoroughbred in the circus.

"Is that what you call a gentleman, Cotilus? Then being a gentleman is a very complicated affair, Cotilus."

Complicated?

It's the end!

XXI

WHEN I first open my eyes a little in the morning and take in the half light I immediately think of something or other: a face, or a sea-going vessel, or my wife's hand. I never want to wake up properly at such times, and I close my eyes again. But my outlandish thoughts give me no peace. I see part of the sky, or my own arm, or a chair, and I ask myself: 'What's that?' 'Oh,' I think, 'it's just the sky, or your arm, or a chair.' I open my eyes wider and look elsewhere, understand at last where I am and what it's all about, and I say to myself: 'Well, there it is. You're alive.'

All right, so I'm still alive. What do I do next? The thing I'd best like would be to close my eyes again, and think of the boat, the face, the white feminine flesh. But by then it's too late and I'm awake.

'All right, get up then,' I think. 'That's the obvious thing to do. But why? What for?'

Yesterday just before I went to sleep I had a headache,

so I read, wrote, thought. . . . But the last thing I thought of was: so you had a headache again!

Who can get rid of it for me? Who can give me anything against it? Where's it leading to?

Perhaps to something different. Perhaps to an animal. Or to Cassius, to Claudia, or to the Emperor.

'All right,' I think to myself, and then I get up.

But the idea worries me. In fact, to be truthful, it's my greatest worry. How does it come about that every morning I wake up with the same obsessive idea that I have to get up? Why? To what purpose? Nothing changes on that account. As far as I'm concerned I might just as well lie on there. But I say to myself: 'So you've woken up again? You're alive. That isn't an accident, so do your part, at least: get up.' And so I get up.

What next? Well, I have a second worry. I find myself a bit odd. The room looks absurd to me. The sun is too strong. I have to yawn. The floor isn't as clean as it might be. I've got ingrowing toenails. And, above all, I haven't any joy in living any more.

'We'll see about that,' I think.

What are we going to see about?

That I'm still there, and alive?

All right, so what about it? What next?

I think of Eleazar. I don't think of him a moment too early. I could have thought of him long ago, but it seems to me that this is just the right moment to think of him, because he can help me get dressed. Is that all right with him? Perhaps his ideas are somewhere else: back again in Judea—or wherever it is he goes at nights. . . .

What do I care? It's my place to do the thinking, not his. Very well, so Eleazar comes. Supposing he didn't come? There would be three possibilities: He is ill, he's dead, or he has run away. If he's ill I fetch the doctor. If he's dead I have him buried. If he has run away I call the police. It's a small world and a narrow life.

I wash myself. Why? To keep myself clean? I'm not really as dirty as all that anyway. To wake myself up? But I'm awake already. To keep myself healthy? I've got to die anyway, and it doesn't really matter when now.

Sometimes I'm afraid of dying. But I'm just as much afraid after I've washed.

I get dressed, and Eleazar helps me into my things.

"Did you have a good night, master?"

"Quite good, thank you. And you?"

"Yes, master. Thank you."

And then: "Do you feel quite well this morning, master?"

"Yes, thank you." I haven't any aches and pains at the moment.

"And how do you feel this morning, Eleazar?"

"Oh, very well, thank you, master."

Another pause in which I think of something or other, perhaps Rome outside the window, or Judea way back in the past, of the sun, of that cat . . . .

And Eleazar thinks too, of something or other. How should I know what he's thinking about? In any case, I ask him.

"Oh, nothing, master," he says.

"But nonsense, Eleazar," I persist, "everyone's thinking of something or other all the time. So tell me what you're thinking of."

"I really wasn't thinking of anything, master. Really I wasn't."

"Where were you last night?"

"In the house, master."

77

"Is that true?"

"I don't quite understand you, master."

"Well, you might have gone out, for example."

"Why, master?"

How should I know? But I might have said: "Because you've often been out before. Perhaps you find it too boring to stay in the house with me; because I'm deaf, and my wife is dead, and you haven't any interest in me any more. No doubt you've found yourself other interests."

I could have said all that, but I didn't. I just said: "Oh, I just got the idea."

"Yes, it's true," said Eleazar. "All sorts of ideas come into one's head."

As my getting dressed approaches completion so my confidence increases, and I feel like a Governor. Eleazar is kneeling before me carefully arranging the folds of my toga. The sight of his bent back makes me straighten mine. In my spine I'm still a Governor at such moments.

But when I'm alone the Governor disappears, and then I'm all sorts of other things; for example, I'm married. I go into my wife's room, feel stuffs, say "Good morning," and imagine that she answers. I look at an arm-band of hers, get pleasure out of it; and go on playing that game until sooner or later I think: 'You're no longer quite normal.'

That upsets me, and then I go out of the room and have the journal fetched, because I think that to occupy myself in that way is something quite "normal"; but before long I'm getting irritable about the writing errors, and wondering whether the bad grammar, which distorts the sense, is the fault of the editor or due to the carelessness of the copyist slaves. But, in any case, it annoys me so much that I soon get tired of that occupation.

'They're mad too,' I think.

What shall I do?

It really isn't simple. I sit down in my arm-chair, close my eyes and talk to myself.

"Well, how are you then?"

"Thank you," I reply. "Quite well."

Pause.

A conversation like that is a bit difficult to keep up. With someone else you can go on talking more easily.

"The sun's shining at the moment," I say. "Do you think it's going to stay fine?"

"I really don't know . . . ."

"Well, I mean, it's nice now."

"Yes, it's nice now."

Pause.

Golden dust is dancing in the sunlight. I clear my throat, and I imagine that with the next breath I take the particles of dust will be drawn into my lungs; and as I'm always a bit scared of that I breathe very softly for a while.

'That will do perfectly well,' I think.

And now?

I ask myself: "How's Claudia, by the way?"

"Oh, she's quite well, thank you. She's got plenty of time and lots of friends. She's very considerate where I'm concerned you know. The fact is she's very fond of me. She likes to be with me . . . ."

"I don't want to say anything that would be too exaggerated, but . . ."

And I go on deceiving myself for a while, and it's quite agreeable.

But in the end it doesn't amuse me any more, and I have to cast around for something else.

'Perhaps you could start writing something,' I think. 'How about it?'

But there's no reaction to that.

"Now, get a move on!" I say to myself sharply.

But after I've bullied myself like that a depressing thought pops up: 'Why? What's the point? What's the use of your writing?'

That does take the wind out of my sails, and I haven't any urge to write any more. But something's got to be done. Then I get very formal with myself and think:

'You've woken up; you've got up; you've washed and dressed and talked to your slave; you've read the journal, thought about your wife and talked to yourself. So what now?'

But no ideas come. Then I read Horace and wonder whether he was a good man, even whether he was really a great man. Perhaps he was merely a careerist and a poltroon. After all, it is a bit odd when a man who himself deserted praises heroes. *Who*, *how* and *what* is a a hero? And must heroes be praised? And who ought to do it? Themselves? And would they be heroes then? Who else is to do it? Some civilian who never smelt blood? When Horace deserted wasn't he perhaps a hero precisely on that account? And aren't there a good many warriors who pass as brave because they're too cowardly to desert?

My thoughts are like a dog chasing its own tail all the time without ever getting tired of the silly business. And now I've brought myself to the point where the headaches start.

'It's your own fault,' I think.

80

I darken the room and wait. Perhaps the headache will go away again. Sometimes I drop off to sleep whilst I'm waiting.

I sit there and think; think that I haven't a wife any more, no children, no profession, no work, no occupation, nothing to do; and can't see any sense or any purpose in life, and have no aim or any objective.

A baker lives more usefully because at least he bakes bread.

Does he?

He sells the murderer bread just before the murderer kills his victim.

A far-fetched example perhaps?

Of course.

But all the same, the victim is dead.

Socrates goes to the banquet. He sits down and remains silent. The people around him are talking, arguing, getting excited. They drink and he remains silent. The wine gives them rare, daring and wonderful ideas. Socrates looks on. He sees them drinking and getting noisier and quarrelsome, or silent. He drinks and remains silent.

And at last, after a night of drinking, the sun rises again. The companions of Socrates are sprawled on the floor sleeping off their hangovers. He empties his goblet, gets up and goes to the fountain, washes himself and then delivers a lecture to his pupils on the soul of man.

When I have no headache the day seems longer. But it's no different on that account. I think over things longer, read a bit more, and close my eyes later.

Is that so very important?

Sometimes I make a point of finding out whether

Eleazar is in the house. If I find he's there I say to myself: "Well, that's all right." And if he isn't I say: "That doesn't matter either."

And then perhaps I try to go to sleep; count up to a thousand, try to distract my thoughts, tell the Emperor just what I really think about him, or pat the flanks of cow after cow in my mind. But perhaps the best thing is obstinately to keep on thinking the same thought; for instance, patting cows: you raise your hand and hold it out until she licks it; then you stroke her broad forehead, pat her flat cheeks, tickle her under the chin . . . Then you do it again: hold out your hand and wait for her to lick it, stroke her forehead, pat her cheeks, tickle her under the chin . . . .

At some point or other you just drop off.

Incidentally, my headaches have developed a new technique: if I draw an imaginary line between the left side of my forehead and the beginning of my neck, then the centre of the pain lies in about the middle of that line. As soon as I cough it twitches at that spot. That's hysterical, of course, but it hurts all the same. Let those damned Rationalists who've got the nerve to say that a normal man just doesn't bother to think of such things tell me where the normal man begins and where he ends.

Whatever you do don't become normal, Pilate my friend; if you did you wouldn't be able to gargle any more without swallowing the water down the wrong way.

XXII

I REALLY deceived myself to the top of my bent just now. What I wrote about Claudia just isn't true. As soon as I can pluck up courage enough I'll destroy those notes. I didn't love her; the fact is I plagued her to death.

I take it that I make a feeble impression physically; my body is anything but strong and vigorous, but, oho, I'm a perfectionist in tormenting.

To feel sorry for myself now is really quite shameless. Now that Claudia is dead . . . (Worms in the flesh, decomposing skin, lumps of clay between the breasts. Earwigs, crawling things, rats. Scrabbling ants and mice that have lost their way. Young snakes, and black crawling beetles . . . Poor Claudia!)

No, I really didn't love her. And I never thought she would die before me.

But if she were to come to me now, for one day, or even only for one hour, I would take her in my arms and hold her tight, for a day or an hour, and keep telling her: "I love you."

Yes, that's what I would do; I really would.

But the real thing isn't what a man *would* do, but what a man *has* done.

And what did I do?

"Did you sleep well?" she would ask.

"Yes, thank you."

Or: "Are you worrying about anything?"

"What should I be worrying about? What gives you that idea? Don't keep on asking so many questions."

Or: "You look a little pale."

"One does sometimes."

Pause.

"Is it all right if I clear the table now?"

I wouldn't reply at all to that one. Of course it was all right. All the same those senseless questions, and what for? Just for the sake of saying something. And then she would sit there looking over at me and waiting for me to say something. But I just didn't choose to.

"All right then," perhaps I would say finally. "Clear the table if you want to."

And so at last she clears the table.

"Do you want anything?"

"No, thank you. Nothing at all."

I can feel that she's sorry I don't want anything. I read the journal.

She doesn't know what to do; she often doesn't know what to do. And because she sits there silently, doing nothing, it irritates me, but I don't say anything either; I control myself.

"I suppose you've become indifferent to me," she says at last. I make no reply to that. I prefer not to hear such remarks.

Pause.

"I had a strange dream last night," she says after a while.

I go on reading and make no comment. It appears that the Emperor is insisting on his idea of making the unwedded state punishable. I don't think it will work myself. I wonder who advised him? A, or B, or perhaps

C. His advisers seem to get more and more stupid as time goes on. "Oh, did you?" I say at last.

"Yes, I dreamt that an owl came to me, perched on that chair, looked at me for a long time and then said . . ."

He really is a fool. If we must have popular policies then let's have them with music, drums rolling, speeches and demagogic aphorisms and slogans to encourage them: "You too a good citizen and a father!" for example or "Happy children, happy mothers!" Or something of the sort. Persuasion by all means, but certainly not force. You just can't tell a twenty-five-year-old man he's got to get married, or else . . . But Claudia was talking about her dream still:

"And then the owl became aggressive and came towards me . . ."

"Really?" I remark.

She looks at me.

"You haven't been listening," she says.

"Of course I was listening. What are you trying to start now?"

She makes no reply. 'Oh dear! Now she's insulted,' I think. 'What for?'

But that article annoys me.

"Don't make such a face," I said.

In the end she got up and went out. I was sorry about that.

"Why are you always so impatient with her?" I reproached myself. "It's always the same. Now she's out there with her hands to her face, crying. I'll get up and go to her."

But I couldn't manage it. I'd like to be nice to her, to go to her and take her hand. But I can never manage it. Now why is that?

"Get up right now and go to her," I would say to myself. "Well?"

But I didn't, of course. 'Perhaps she'll come back of her own accord,' I think. 'I'll count up to ten . . . No, up to fifteen. And if she hasn't come back by that time I'll get up and go to her.'

"One, two, three, four . . ."

A bit childish really. A grown man sits there and counts on his fingers before he can summon up enough courage to go to his wife and say amiably: "Well, what's the matter?"

But that's how it always is. I always have to be the one who gives way. I didn't do anything to her, didn't say a cross word, nothing. She ought to have some husbands I know! They come home drunk, make scenes, go with other women and beat their own . . . She doesn't know when she's well off. No, really, nothing's happened at all.

I pick up the journal again and decide that it's beneath my dignity to bother my head about such trivialities. I've got other things to worry about, more important things to think of. Ridiculous! "Now," I say to myself. "Just read your journal in peace and forget the whole thing."

All right, so I go on reading.

I read headlines and words and sentences and paragraphs . . . And after a while I ask myself: "Well, what have you read so far?"

Nothing really. I've just strung letters together and made words of them, that's all. 'She isn't coming back,' I think. 'Perhaps I'll count up to ten after all? Very well.'

"One, two, three, four, five."

Supposing I do count up to ten, what then? Then I'll go to her and say: "Claudia, please . . ."

But I know already that I shan't go to her. And I

certainly shan't say: "Claudia, please . . ." I know myself
too well for that. I just couldn't get the words over my
lips. If I've got to say something, then I'll say something
quite different. I shall say: "What's the matter with you
now?", or "Are you offended again?", or "What's upset
you this time?"

Brooding over it makes my heart beat harder than it
should. I ask myself what it was that made her go out
like that, but I can't remember any more what it was.
Was there any good reason at all?

And I tell myself it's foolish to be angry and not even
to know why.

So, steady now, calm down. I'll get up and go to her.
But there she is; I can hear her coming. I stand there with
my left ear cocked towards the door. That's the ear I
hear better with. And I listen. No, I must have been
mistaken. I might have known, really. She never comes,
never. She's stronger than I am, I know that.

'But I can be as obstinate as you can,' I think to myself.
'We'll see about that.'

I try to give myself courage by whistling carelessly. I
don't know what I'm whistling. But, in any case, we'll
see about that.

'Of course though,' I have to admit to myself, 'she
doesn't have it easy with you. You're sometimes very
difficult, and that's a fact. You've got your little ways.
And don't forget you're half-deaf. And you've got a will
of your own too. That's all true,' I admit to myself. 'And
you're not very cheerful either. People say you're complicated.' (People! Damn people! They've got a hundred
and one faults themselves, but they think they've got the
right to condemn others for their faults. "Pilate is a
complicated fellow," they say. Don't they think they're

87

complicated for me? Do they think it's so easy for me to understand them? For me *they're* complicated. And that's that!)

But she really isn't coming back.

"One, two, three . . . seven, eight, nine, ten. Right! Go to her now," I say to myself. "Pull yourself together and just go."

But supposing she's gone out: for a walk, to the Tiber? She wouldn't *do* anything to herself would she?

I call Eleazar and tell him to ask my wife to come to me.

"Certainly, master," he replies. Everything's certain for people like that.

It seems a long time before he comes back. What shall I do? I force myself to think of the Emperor, or snake poison, of the perversions of the Jews, or of Tiberius.

Eleazar comes back and says the mistress is not feeling well and begs to be excused.

I ought really to have expected that. I'm annoyed at my own stupidity, and feel like letting Eleazar bear the brunt of my anger, but I control myself.

I'm alone again. What now?

Headaches. I *was* fond of you, Claudia.

XXIII

Go on then: I did love her. I didn't much care for eating with other people. When she was out of the house I couldn't concentrate on reading. I'd wake up at nights and whisper: "Are you there, Claudia?" And if she went away I used to feel upset. Yes, I certainly loved her.

Once we came home from a party, and she said: "You didn't take any notice of me the whole evening."

"Oh, really!"

"Yes. You didn't look at me once, and you didn't say a single word to me."

"Well . . ."

"You can talk to R. for hours on end. You seem to have plenty to talk about then. But you can sit with me for hours and not find anything to say."

"I really can't understand you."

"No, that's probably true, but let me tell you one thing . . ."

"All right! All right! So you're right."

"No, it's not a question of my being right or not. But when you don't even see how bored I am . . ."

"Then that means I don't love you any more, I know."

"You even admit it!"

"Don't twist what I say so. I just said . . ."

"I don't twist what you say. I won't have you say that, do you hear? In any case, you didn't say a word to me. It's you that brings that up again."

"I'm not bringing anything up."

"Yes, you are."

"All right, well how then?"

"Are you cross-examining me? What do you think you're doing?"

"I'm just asking you what you mean when you say I keep bringing up things that aren't true. Please forgive the question, and answer it."

"I never heard such a thing!"

"Well, you're hearing it now."

"We've been married for years, but I have to listen to this sort of squabble again and again."

"I'm sorry, but I have to listen to it too. Though, of course, I'm deaf."

"Then say something. Say: 'Come, let's make it up!'"

I wouldn't. Why me?

"Look at me," she said.

I wouldn't. Why should I?

"Don't you want to?"

"Just as you please," I said.

She looked at me.

"You have no heart," she said. "That's what's the matter with you. And I shall never get used to it. I shall never understand it."

"Well, all right then: you'll never understand it. And after that?"

"I realize that it doesn't matter to you."

"Gradually nothing's beginning to matter to me, and that's a fact."

"Of course! You also didn't care when I had to stay alone for days in Caesarea."

"Oh, you're not going to bring that up again surely?"
Silence.

"Are you going to sit there much longer like that?"

"Does it disturb you?"
Silence.

"If there were only something I could do; someone to whom I could go."

"Now that's exactly what I was waiting for!"

"Well, do you think that an evening like this is any pleasure for me?"

"No, I don't think anything of the sort. But you seem to think it gives me some pleasure."

90

"It looks like it."

"Don't say things like that. I won't have it."

"Really? So you won't have it? And I won't have you saying I twist everything round."

"All right, so you don't twist everything round. I'm sorry. You're the embodiment of truth; and the worst of it is, you really believe it yourself."

"You needn't be sarcastic."

"I'll decide whether I need to be sarcastic or not, if you don't mind. But if you like I won't be sarcastic; I won't say anything at all."

"I'm certainly used to that."

"Well, there you are! You get used to everything in time. You even get used to a wife who says her husband is a drinker."

"What's that got to do with it? No one said a word about that."

"I think I'm entitled to say it, or have you any objection?"

"I have no objection to anything."

"That's nice of you, I must say."

Silence. (A moment or two, an hour, half the night —it just depends.)

Then one starts up again. Perhaps me.

"Have you lost your voice?"

"You haven't been saying a great deal yourself."

Or maybe she starts:

"We just sit around here"—with a sigh.

"Do you think I'm not sitting here too?"

It doesn't matter who starts, and it doesn't matter who answers.

And then?

We attack each other with silence. And then perhaps

I say: "Would you like something to drink?"

"Why do you ask?"

"Because then I'd get up and get something to drink."

"Oh, I see."

"You needn't say 'Oh, I see' like that. I'd just get up and go and get something; that's all."

"It would be the first time."

"It wouldn't be the first time at all, but never mind; just as you please: for the first time I'd get up and go and fetch something to drink."

"Do you feel thirsty then?"

"That's not the point at the moment. I asked you a civil question, and I was hoping—in vain I suppose—to get a civil answer. Let me try again. Would you like something to drink?"

She stared at me with pain in her eyes. I never could stand her looking at me like that.

"How horribly logical men are!" she said.

"That's true, I suppose. Men are logical. But 'men' is a very general expression. All right, then I'm not asking you whether you'd like anything to drink."

Silence.

"Can't you really make a move towards me?"

I didn't answer that, and I didn't look at her.

"You can be terribly brutal."

"If you like."

"You stand in your own light."

"Agreed."

"Can't you behave any differently?"

"How would you like me to behave?"

"I'd like you to take my hand and tell me you love me."

"That's just what I wish *you* would do."

"I can't always be the one who gives way."

"Neither can I."

Pause.

"Very well, I'm going now."

"All right."

She got up and waited for a word from me. 'Aha!' I thought.

"Well," I said, "I thought you said you were going."

"You seem to want to get rid of me."

"I don't mind, but you did say you were going."

And now she's dead. I love you, Claudia. And I'm alone. I haven't anyone. And when I had you I tormented you—all the same I really do love you. If only you'd knock the journal out of my hand at the breakfast table, and shout at me as you use to. I'd give anything for that again: an eye, an ear; anything you like. But she's dead.

The death of one's nearest is like losing a limb, a kind of amputation. Every day I am amputated anew. Sometimes the whole body seems to disappear and all that remains is the pain lying in wait above the spinal column.

XXIV

I was born in Rome. I have good reason not to talk too much about my parents.

My father was an advocate. I had neither brother nor sister.

My education was, as far as I can remember, quite

normal. I was an average pupil; though I made no friendships with others of my own age. From a child on I had a tendency to choose older companions. And now I am a widower.

My wife is dead.

I can't establish any sort of contact with heroes. They bore me and I find most of them stupid. They never even see a problem, and if they should by any chance, then they lie themselves round it. I prefer the unsuccessful. They are heroic because they're forced to be, not out of sheer bombast.

Occupation: ex-Governor.

Not exceptionally gifted. Almost deaf.

References: my slave.

Material situation: tolerable.

Special knowledge: country and people of the Near East, languages, alcoholica.

Hobby horses: Palestine, Jews, cats, Socrates, the late Emperor, religious hallucinations. And in addition I'm thoroughly acquainted with the headache in all its forms.

Summa summarum: suitable guinea pig for headaches; conditionally suitable as a neurotic type with a particular tendency to vegetative distonie; unsuitable as a human being.

Question: what do you do with two eyes, two arms, two legs, one deaf ear, one nose, a head, and, as far as I'm concerned, a reasonably functioning brain?

Answer: you exist, and go on existing.

But what do you do about the diagnosis: unsuitable as a human being?

I'll tell you: you take a deep breath; don't look too closely; shut your half-deaf ear; take life as it comes; head forward, muscles of your backside tight, tread downwards, bow upwards, push to the left, help push to the right, keep open your line of retreat; don't think, don't act, don't cough sensibly, and don't urinate suitably.

Just live naturally.

Naturally?

XXV

Talk with Barabbas:

Pilate: "You were sentenced to death I believe; how did that come about?"

Barabbas: "No one knows that better than you."

"But I'd like to hear your version."

"Because the Tabernacle revolt failed."

"You mean the revolt in the town?"

"Yes."

"You were a robber?"

"I was a revolutionary."

"Who was the ring-leader?"

"I was."

"Where are your companions?"

"They were cut down."

"Were you the only survivor?"

"No, there were two others."

"How did that happen?"

"You know that yourself."

"I'm asking you."

"Because your Roman soldiers wanted to satisfy their vanity."

"You mean as a deterrent?"

"No, I mean as an outward demonstration of the power of Rome."

"Do you really believe that?"

"Yes, I do."

"Were you wounded?"

"No, I was not."

"And your companions?"

"One of them was. Your soldiers nursed him back to health and then he was killed."

"You mean that he was crucified as a rebel?"

"That's what I mean."

"Do you think the people love you because they imagine you're a hero?"

"The Party of Freedom cares something about me."

"Isn't the Party of Freedom the people then?"

"Only a few love freedom."

"Amongst your people perhaps. But every Roman would die without freedom."

"Because you're doing quite well out of it."

"We're not doing very well out of it by accident; we fought for our prosperity and freedom."

"That was my aim too."

" 'Was'? Have you abandoned it then?"

"Would I answer you otherwise?"

"I'm asking the questions, not you. Why do you think you were defeated?"

"We were betrayed."

"Really?"

"I'm not lying."

"As a political leader you just have to lie, but there's no need to lie to me."

"Are you a political leader?"

"I'm asking the questions, I told you. Now you know the law, and you know that at the Feast of the Passover a convicted criminal sentenced to death has to be reprieved. But what I want to know is: why did the people choose you?"

"That was very clever of you."

"Clever of me?"

"Yes, to persuade the people of your liberality."

"Wasn't I liberal then?"

"Well..."

"Go on, what do you mean? Answer."

"As I said, you demonstrated your liberality to the people."

"But you don't really believe it?"

"I didn't say that."

"Well, what is it you want to say?"

"Don't you remember?"

"Let me see, you were to be crucified on the eve of the Jewish festival, weren't you?"

"Yes, that's right."

"After we had defeated you and your comrades."

"You didn't defeat us."

"Who did then?"

"We were betrayed."

"Very well, have it your own way. What happened then?"

"The people were indignant. The law forbids not only executions but even legal proceedings on the eve of feast days."

"The law of Augustus did, but Tiberius is the Emperor now, and he has different ideas on the subject."

"Aha!"

"What do you mean by that?"

"Nothing."

"Answer truthfully. Do you understand?"

"Yes. I was only wondering whether the Romans always thought like their Emperor for the time being."

"The Emperor is not 'for the time being'. But you shall have your answer; in the form of questions. Did you and your friends show any consideration for the nature of the day? Did the Freedom Party bother about it in the least? Did any of you show the slightest consideration for your God, for the law, and for the Roman soldiers?"

"We wanted to be free."

"What I asked you was whether you and your friends showed any consideration for the nature of the day?"

"No, we didn't."

"And would you have shown any consideration on the following feast days?"

"We hadn't any particular plans."

"So you hadn't any particular plans?"

"No long-term plans."

"What I asked you was whether you would have kept quiet over the Feast of the Passover."

"I can't say."

"I see. And, tell me, how many pilgrims come into Jerusalem for the Feast of the Passover?"

"A great many."

"Make an estimate."

"A few hundred thousand."

"Very well. And now supposing that you had repeated your insurrection, what would have happened?"

"There were too few of us."

"What would have happened? I asked."

"There could have been fighting."

98

"Could have been? You choose your words very carefully."

"I learnt that in Roman dungeons."

"You were there according to due process of law."

"What law?"

"The law of Rome. And therefore . . ."

"To the cross with them! I understand. We're to wail for Rome."

"No, not for Rome, for justice."

"That's a very different matter."

"Not for me." Pause. "Not for me, I said."

"I heard you."

"And what have you got to say?"

"What is the question?"

"How does it come that you can regard rebellion as a just thing? Don't you know that it's *lèse-majesté*?"

"Yes, I do."

"Well?"

"What was allowed according to law under Augustus is *lèse-majesté* under Tiberius. How should I know where I stand?"

"By reading the laws."

"I do read the laws, but the judges interpret them differently."

"Do you mean me?"

"No, not particularly."

"Well, who then?"

"Just the judges. Just judges in general."

XXVI

"How did you come to join the Freedom Party?"

"My father was a revolutionary before me."

"Where was that?"

"In the neighbourhood of Arbela."

"Did he lose his life?"

"Yes, in the struggle against Herod."

"How exactly?"

"Herod's soldiers were lowered down the rock face in baskets and they smoked them out of their holes."

"Herod wiped out most of the rebels, didn't he?"

"Yes. Only a few were left."

"Who was the founder of your party?"

"Judas, a Galilean."

"When did he live?"

"Soon after Archelaus."

"He stirred you up against the payment of the poll tax, didn't he?"

"He taught us that it was a sin against God to pay taxes to the Goyim."

"And you believed him?"

"Yes, I did and do believe him."

"You had three parties already; why did you found a fourth? Weren't the Pharisees nationalistic enough for you? What's the difference between you?"

"You know that already."

"Answer my question."

"Very well. The Pharisees are tacticians. They want to collaborate with you just as long as they think they're not strong enough to overthrow you."

"And you think that's a cowardly thing to do? Or not?"

B. made no answer.

"You mean that the difference is that your party recruits hooligans and bandits to carry out insurrection and murder. And that's the difference between your party and the Pharisees?"

B. still made no answer.

"Haven't you courage enough to answer?"

"Between you and me, sir, there's no such thing as cowardice and courage."

"What is there then?"

"Just question and answer."

"When did the Pharisees want to rise?"

"After the coming of the Messiah."

"Why not sooner?"

"Because they considered you too strong. And because they remembered only too well the slaughter under Pompey, Sosius and Varus."

"And didn't you remember it too?"

"Oh yes, we remembered it all right."

"Well?"

"We didn't mind."

"Do you mind now?"

"Yes, I do."

"Why?"

"You don't believe in the Messiah, and therefore I'd sooner not talk to you about it."

"You carried out plundering on quite a large scale."

"War always lives off the land."

"You set fire to houses."

"The houses of traitors."

"You attacked and kidnapped innocent people."

"We needed them as hostages to exchange for our own people."

"How many bands of you are there?"

"A number."

"Give a figure."

"I'm no longer a revolutionary."

"But you know all the same."

"No."

"Shall I have you scourged?"

B. made no answer.

(No punishment, because the man is more useful to me if I can talk to him.)

"During my period of office so far there have been two insurrections. You took part in one of them. Why do you now come to me and ask for protection? Do you need protection? And why should I believe you?"

"The revolutionaries will want to revenge themselves on me. I owe them my life."

"You made arrangements for them to be there and shout you free, didn't you?"

"I was a leader. I didn't need to make any arrangements for them to be there. They came of their own accord."

"Very well, but what's happened since?"

"Everything has changed since then. He died for me, and I am no longer the same."

"He? Do you mean Jesus of Nazareth?"

"Yes, the Messiah."

"Do you really believe that he was the Messiah?"

"Yes, I do."

102

"And so now the revolutionaries regard you as a traitor, is that it?"

"They say I disappointed them. I should be on my guard."

"Are you afraid?"

"Not very much."

"You mean they think you've become a friend of Rome's; and you don't much care for that?"

B. made no reply.

"You don't much care for that? I asked you."

"They don't understand me."

"And what about me? Can I trust you?"

"That is your affair."

"You never crucified anyone, did you?"

"Never."

"But you chopped off their heads?"

"Not before binding their eyes first."

Eleazar came in a moment or two ago and brought me a message from Stephanio. It reads: "Be on your guard against Eleazar. He is an enemy of the State. Further details verbally."

What am I supposed to make of that? Who isn't an enemy of the State nowadays? What does it matter to me? Perhaps it's just that Stephanio wants to borrow some more money.

XXVII

P.: "You knew that I wanted to take funds from the Temple Treasury?"

B.: "Yes."

"And so I suppose you think I'm a thief?"

"No."

"Why did you give the signal for insurrection?"

"Because the Temple was about to be desecrated."

"By me?"

"Yes."

"I needed the money to build a useful water conduit, you knew that perfectly well."

"Yes, of course."

"Well then, why do you talk about the desecration of the Temple? Am I a swindler perhaps?"

"That was God's money."

"God's money?"

"Yes, certainly."

"You really are fanatical."

"No, we just believe firmly. That's all."

"You rose against Sabinus for the same reason. Is that right?"

"Yes, the same reason."

"And against Heliodorus too?"

"Yes, against Heliodorus too."

"You think I would have been wiser to have taken that into account?"

"I didn't say that."

"But you think so! Do you seriously think that I could possibly have had any interest in provoking an insurrection in connection with the Feast of the Passover? At a time when hundreds of thousands would have been against me! Perhaps you think I'm stupid?"

"No, I don't."

"Well, what is it you have against me?"

"Nothing."

"But you think I ought not to have taken the money?"

"As things were you could afford to."

"What do you mean, 'as things were'?"

"Because we had been betrayed to you."

"What makes you so sure of that?"

"I'm not just sure of it; I *know* it."

"Your answers are frequently insolent, don't you think?"

"No, not insolent, just frank and truthful."

"Well, what makes you think that you were betrayed?"

"If you are trying to make a fool of me I won't answer any more. I am not afraid of scourging. It is nothing new to me."

"Do you really think I'm trying to make a fool of you?"

"I think I do."

"What makes you think that?"

"Because you knew our plans as well as we knew them ourselves."

"Yes, I did. That's quite true."

B. was silent.

"You've nothing to say to that?"

"Nothing."

"Does this discussion upset you?"

"No."

"Is that because you think you've seen the Messiah in the meantime?"

"I have seen the Messiah in the meantime."

"About those traitors, do you know them?"

"I know where they're to be found."

"Namely?"

"I can't mention any names."

"Do you mean you don't know any names?"

"That's true, I don't know any names."

"But what about their positions, their aims, their party?"

"Oh yes, I know all that."

"Well?"

"One or two highly-placed Pharisees and a few scared Saducees."

"You're sure you're not mistaken?"

"I hardly think so."

"But Pharisees and Saducees are like cat and dog together. And now suddenly they're supposed to be acting in concert. How do you think that could come about?"

"The end justifies the means."

"What end exactly?"

"They want to keep their riches, their position, their privileges, their possessions and their opportunist beliefs. They want power and influence on the cheap, and contemptible prosperity."

"And what about your people? What did you want?"

"We wanted freedom."

"Just what sort of freedom?"

"There's only one kind of freedom."

"And what does that look like?"

B. was silent.

"Didn't you hear my question?"

"Yes, I did."

"Well, answer it then."

B. still remained silent.

"You haven't courage enough to give it a name. Very well, I'll describe it for you: your kind of freedom means the overthrow of Rome, the death of my soldiers, my own death, the death of my wife—in fact death and death and death. Isn't that what your freedom would look like?"

B. still remained silent.

"Are you going to answer me or not?"

"We wanted freedom for all men."

"All men?"

"Yes, all men."

"But death for all Roman soldiers?"

"Yes."

"And that's what you call freedom!"

"All freedom begins with killing."

"Does it? We never put anyone to death without good reason."

"There's a cross on every hill."

"The cross of a criminal."

"No, the cross of a fighter for freedom."

"Do you really think that?"

"Yes, I do."

"What sort of freedom did the crucified want then?"

"Aren't we turning round in circles now?"

"I know. I *want* us to turn round in circles. I'm anxious to see who can stand it longer."

"You, of course."

"Why me?"

"Because you're the one who asks the questions. That

gives you the advantage. And I have to answer, and that puts me at a disadvantage. And the last question, which must remain unanswered, leaves me bested. Before the supposed objective you just trip me up and I'm on the floor."

"You're very pat with all your answers. Where did you learn that?"

"From disputing with the Pharisees."

"Do you know why your plan was bad?"

"You mean the plan for the insurrection?"

"Yes."

"Perhaps not."

"Very well, I'll tell you. It was because you proposed to adopt tactics which had already failed against Sabinus. Plans must be new if they are to have any hope of success."

"I didn't know anything about the former plans."

"Come, come!"

"I didn't. I really didn't."

"But I did."

B. was silent.

"From which you can conclude how important strategy is."

"Particularly when you add treachery to it, yes."

"You had gathered your people at three different points, hadn't you?"

"Yes."

"Around the Governor's tribune in the lower citadel, at the burnt-offerings altar, and on the Siloe."

"Correct."

"And where were you?"

"At the altar."

"Why not at the tribune? Why not near me?"

"Because the people there were less important. They

weren't even armed. At a given signal they were to petition you against the seizure of the Temple money, and quite generally to create a disturbance. They were just hangers on; they weren't real revolutionaries."

"And when *I* gave the signal, what did you make of that?"

"The first thing I thought of was treachery, of course."

"You hadn't noticed anything before that?"

"I then saw the climbing ropes prepared at the Hall of Pillars."

"And how did you react to that?"

"I was furious."

"You didn't even fight then?"

"No."

"You just let yourselves be taken by surprise?"

"Treachery always paralyses."

"My soldiers didn't even use their swords."

"I know."

"You see, I had forbidden them to."

"Had you?"

"Yes, but you don't seem to find anything strange about that?"

"No."

"You don't think it would have been an easy matter for my soldiers to slaughter the lot of you?"

"Oh yes, I do."

"But I wanted to avoid bloodshed. That doesn't seem to make any impression on you."

"It was very clever of you."

"Just clever of me?"

"The behaviour of a mob of people driven mad by desperate anger is incalculable."

"They would have been destroyed."

"And quite a few Roman soldiers too."
"A soldier must always reckon with that."
"But you haven't very many soldiers."

XXVIII

. . . .
. . . .[1]

And I can't get over the injustice of my recall either. I
was good enough as long as the Empire found me useful.
It wasn't true that the Emperor regarded the demands
of the Jews as reasonable. If he says that now, he's lying.
The Jews put forward new demands every day. They
complained about every Governor, and that wasn't
because any particular Governor didn't suit them, but
because they wanted no Governor at all. At the slightest
excuse they sent petitions to the Emperor, despatched
threatening letters, and employed one of the best advocates in Rome to represent their interest. And I was on my
own. I hadn't any real power; I hadn't enough money,
and I hadn't enough soldiers. The tactics the Emperor
adopted were very simple. He just gave them his little
finger and promised them a different Governor, a better
Governor, a Governor with whom they'd be able to get
on. And what difference did it make? None at all. When
I arrived to take up my new duties I was the "better"
Governor, and when I was recalled, V., who took my
place, was the "better" Governor. It was as simple as

[1] The first few lines rendered illegible by Pilate. L.P.B.

that. And nothing changed. He crucified people too. He needed money too. And, as I heard subsequently, three times as much as I did. So what was the point in recalling me?

"For tactical reasons."

But precisely there lies the great danger. The Jews have learnt by this time that they hold the Governor in the palm of their hand. They know perfectly well: fifteen or twenty petitions, and he's ready for the drop.

Naturally they exploit the situation. And who can blame them? What is the real situation? The Governor arrives in Judea to rule the Jews in the interests of Rome. And naturally he doesn't rule as the Jews want him to rule; so Rome recalls him.

That's what the tactics of the Emperor amount to, and they're just idiotic. He's incapable of seeing beyond the end of his nose.

I wonder why he leaves me in Rome. Does he prefer to have me near enough for him to lay his hands on if he wants to? Why doesn't he send me into banishment? There's nothing to prevent him, and if he did there's hardly a soul who'd be put out, much less protest. Eleazar told me the other day that a friend had advised him to leave me. Why? he had asked. And he was told that it would be better for him to be the lowest slave of Cassius rather than the highest slave of Pilate. Why? he repeated. "Why?" the other echoed. "You must be a fool."

Sometimes I don't feel all too comfortable in my skin myself. And in addition, on account of my deafness I've become a little mistrustful. I often imagine that people are talking about me. I look at their lips and try to read the words as they speak them. 'They're talking about me,' I think. 'They're saying: "Look, there's Pilate! He's in disgrace now, you know. He won't last much longer." '

And afterwards I happen to find out that they've been talking about the weather.

But that's the way everybody lives to-day—and not merely because he's deaf! Later on, when the Emperor's dead, when I'm dead, and when Rome no longer exists (and it can't exist much longer because all it cares about nowadays is eating well, drinking heavily, money, women, circuses and sensations) it will appear incredible that in our day people thought only of themselves. That's the only interesting thing about it.

It's rather strange when you know perfectly well that thirty years after your death not a soul will know anything about you.

Stephanio came to see me.

"What's that you're writing?" he asked.

"My memoirs."

"Oh, I'd like very much to read them."

"I'm afraid you can't; they're intended only for me."

"But I'm your friend."

"Yes, of course. But all the same . . ."

At that he was rather annoyed, and he went. I shrugged my shoulders. What can I do about it?

XXIX

Draft:

"DEAR Claudia, since you died everything is very different. I never knew what it meant to be alone. I wake up. Adjust myself to the new day. First thought:

where am I? Second thought: where is Barabbas? (That's the vestige of a dream.) Third thought: she's dead. And I sigh. To start the day like that is hard. The breakfast table is still bare, but Eleazar is just setting it. The bread isn't the same nowadays. It leaves a smell on the hands I don't care for. I am alone. No one says anything. I concentrate my attention on the journal. Then suddenly I think I hear a slight noise. 'There's someone in the room!' I assume, and I get scared. Slowly I turn my head round to see whether there's anyone behind me. But there isn't. Now I get up and search the room. Then I breathe a sigh of relief. 'So you see, you're alone,' I think. But I make quite sure once more, put my ear to the wall, sound the floor, and then listen carefully. But no, there's no one and nothing there. . . . I wait a moment or two and then turn round suddenly, because I've heard something again. A slight sniff. Someone suppressing a cough. But I'm wrong again. There's no one there.

"I'm often wrong now that you're not there. I don't hear properly any more, of course. I don't understand any more either. I walk up and down, stop, keep quiet and listen. Suddenly the silence is eerie, and I realize that there's no one there at all but me. No one in the whole of Rome; no one in the whole of the Empire; no one in the whole world. And then I get scared again. I put my hands to my forehead and press the wrinkles together so violently that it hurts. Then I shake my head to make the ideas fall differently. 'But you're really quite alone,' I think. And I can't stand it any more, so I beat my fists against the wall and shout for Eleazar. 'Eleazar! Eleazar! Eleazar!'

"He comes, of course, looks at me in astonishment, and asks: 'Yes, master. Is anything the matter?'

" 'Yes, there's something the matter all right. Claudia is dead. That's what's the matter,' He stares at me with his silly helpless eyes, and I feel like shouting at him and pummelling him with my fists instead of the wall, but all I say is: 'No, Eleazar, it's all right. There's nothing the matter. You can go.'

"And he goes, of course. He does everything I tell him to. If I said to him 'Go and hang yourself!' he would nod his head and look at me inquiringly: 'Yes, master; where?'

"Of course, I'm being unjust to him. He doesn't know. He doesn't realize how alone I am. I see faces on the street; some of them stupid, some of them ugly; some of them arrogant. And I think: 'Claudia is dead. All these faces, and Claudia's dead.' A little too much pathos perhaps, but that's how I do think. And then in some corner or other of my brain ideas begin to swing their hammers and clear the way for my headache.

"I feel like chatting to you.

"Just imagine, Stephanio . . . You remember Stephanio, don't you? You said you felt he wasn't 'sincere', remember? That was the year before I was appointed. You wore that little coral necklace. Do you remember that? Later on you lost it. I was a bit put out about that, and . . .

"Excuse me, I'm wandering from the point, I must concentrate. I wanted to say: when Stephanio has to play a man suffering from headache what does he do? He puts his hands to his head, presses his temples, makes a face, closes his eyes, groans, rubs his neck, pulls his hair as though he wanted to pull it out in handfuls, groans again, wipes the sweat from his forehead, puts his hands before his face, opens his mouth, shouts, lowers his head . . . And?

"It's all play-acting. When I have a real headache I

114

just sit down and wait. And I don't do anything at all.

"Forgive me. I really wanted to tell you how fond of you I am. But I always say something else. Do you think of me? My headaches have grown worse. I wasn't very good to you; I know that. You mustn't think I'm unwilling to admit it.

"Do you remember when we were on the mountain that time? We went right up to the top and looked into the sky, into the sun, into our own eyes. I can look into your eyes for hours. They're very deep, but translucent right down to the depths, where there are moving plants and colours. And the longer I look into them the more difficult it is for me. I can't stand it any longer. I have to close my eyes. And then it gets dark, and hot under my lids, hot and very prickly, very . . . No, I'm not going to admit that. I mustn't weep. What would things come to if men started to cry like women? I swallow hard, laugh, open my eyes wide in order to force the tears back, and say something jocularly abusive, or: 'Oh, yes, I almost forgot; the Emperor sent you his kind regards!' And I laugh more and more, and see your eyes again. *But that's just what I mustn't do!* The more I love you the deeper I can see into them. The depths disappear, together with the plants and the colours, And I can see deeper, and deeper. And then you do spot my tears and you ask: 'What's the matter?' What's the matter? I just love you, that's all. But instead I say: 'What's the matter? Nothing's the matter. What a silly question! I'm just an idiot. And there aren't any tears.' But you persist: 'What are you crying for then? Why are you so sad?' 'Sad?' I say. 'Who's sad?' 'You are. Do you love me?' 'What!' I exclaim, and I swallow as many tears as I can, 'Love you? What an idea! What makes you think that?' And then you say angrily: 'Let me go then!' 'No,' I say, 'I won't let you alone.' 'But you said you didn't love me.' 'No, I didn't say that at all.'

"I kissed you, and it was warm, and we were alone and we looked into the sky. And Rome and everyone else were centuries away. I kissed you, and you asked: 'Do you like my skin?' And I just laughed. 'Are you happy?' you asked. And I nodded. And then the tears came again. And you cried. And it was my turn to say: 'What are you crying for?' I saw your tears, and your skin, and my hands wanted to stroke it, but they passed over you like a breath. I shall never be so close to you again as that. And now it's all over. 'Come back!' I think. 'Come back!' And you asked: 'What are you thinking about?' 'Oh, nothing,' I replied. 'Do you love me?' 'Yes, I love you.' 'Are you happy?' 'Yes, I'm happy.' 'I can still see tears.' 'I just love you, that's all.' 'And I love you too.' I see your skin. Tiny little pores, and the sun shining on it. The skin on your neck seems to grow transparent in the sun, and the skin of your bosom seems to breathe in the sun. 'I'd like to stroke it,' I think. 'Or just look at it, just look at it.' "

XXX

I WOULD be an ideal subject for the quacks now. Of course, it wouldn't be their job to heal my deafness. I've learned to live quite well with that. Their job would be to give me different thoughts.

But that's just what they couldn't do.

They couldn't do it because they just aren't capable of treating thoughts. They tell me: "Your thoughts *are* just sick." But I say: "*Your* thoughts are sick, and you don't even notice it. And worse still, you regard your two-a-penny sort of brain as the hub of the universe."

"Headaches?" they ask. "Oh, in that case take A. B. C.P.O. herbs. That always helps."

It doesn't, of course. Ever.

XXXI

IF just for an hour I had the power of the gods there are a number of things I would do:

1. Give each human being ten thousand words, and when he had spoken them all he would have to die;

2. Abolish the feeling of power. It just wouldn't exist any more;

3. Make about ten per cent of all animals uncreated: cats, for example. I wouldn't want them to become dependent;

4. I would make slaves either more like animals, or more arrogant than ever;

5. I should force everyone to live backwards. That is to say, not: "I'm alive, what shall I do?" But: "I'm about to die; what have I done?";

6. Make procreation no longer a pleasure. It would be an act of deliberate decision;

7. Make lying different. It would be a lie to shake hands with someone else unwillingly;

8. Experience human beings as fleas, just hopping around;

9. Make pain and pleasure more painful;

10. Make happiness play a bigger role than desire;

11. Deny that there is such a thing as gods in order to prove it;

12. Adjust all hearing to my capacity, i.e. ask three times what is meant;

13. Make crosses and crucify on them all those who don't talk to say something (the Emperor);

14. Make the sex rise at the beautiful, the good and the nice, but not at the exposed;

15. Force the lions to let themselves be tamed;

16. Forbid the lion to become tame;

17. Distribute more headaches so that people begin to notice where it hurts;

18. Attach great pain to great fame;

19. Worship Socrates, although I'm a god;

20. Abolish "who", "when" and "where", and allow only "how" and "why";

21. Make the nights darker; and

22. Wake up my wife.

Fable:

A man sees a lion and goes up to stroke it. The lion strikes him senseless with one blow of its paw. When the man recovers consciousness he says: "But I only wanted to stroke you."

"I'm so sorry," replies the lion, amiably licking the man's hands, but leaving him there to bleed to death.

I've lost three pages of my notes. I've looked

everywhere for them, but without finding them.

If they have been stolen, only two people could possibly have stolen them: Eleazar and Stephanio. And I trust Eleazar.

XXXII

CALLED Eleazar to account:

"Where were you?"

"At the graves, master."

"In the middle of the night?"

"Yes."

"What were you doing there?"

"Nothing."

"You're lying to me."

"I'm not lying, master."

"You leave the house in the middle of the night to go to the graves to do nothing there?"

"Yes, master."

"Are you a bit off your head then?"

"No, master."

"Now come; I want a clear and truthful answer: what were you doing there?"

"Nothing, master."

"Must you always say: 'Yes, master,' 'No, master,' or 'Nothing, master'?"

"Yes, master."

"Now listen to me, my friend. I have received a confidential message which says that you are taking part in nefarious machinations against the State. What have you got to say to that?"

"Nothing, master."

"Is it true then?"

"No, master."

"Well, what is true then?"

Eleazar remained silent.

"Are you going to answer me or not?"

He hesitated, looked at me, didn't seem to know what to say, and finally he said: "Master, I must first ask whether I may speak. I shall be back quickly."

And with that he disappeared.

Nowadays slaves order their masters around. The interesting thing is that they can do only two things really well: tyrannize and obey. But even with their obedience they are tyrannical.

Eleazar has made a "discovery" which is not only quite fantastic but also totally absurd:

There is a God, and he had a son. This son had to die because that's the way his father wanted it, and because all men are bad. This son of God was a Jew, and he was crucified. Not only that, but he was crucified in Judea during my term of office. In other words, I crucified him. In any case, nobody noticed that this fellow was "God".

That is, according to my servant.

Servant?

They can't stand fair treatment. That's what it looks like.

And this madness has now spread even to Rome. It would seem that we're not to be spared anything at all.

XXXIII

Dream:
I HAVE a tremendous head. I am on the street. The people
are passing by. I observe them carefully and say to myself:
they must be able to see that you've got a tremendous head.
But they don't seem to notice it at all. They pass me,
chatting to each other, and I don't seem to be anything
unusual for them. And that makes me think that perhaps
I'm mistaken; perhaps I haven't got a huge head at all.
Perhaps my head is really quite normal? Of course, I must
be mistaken; so I turn into a side street and find a quiet
doorway with the intention of feeling my head. But just
at that moment a young man comes by, sees me, starts,
stops and looks at me. 'What does the fellow want?'
I think. But then he goes on as though nothing at all had
happened. I don't trust him though, for all that. I'm
quite sure he noticed my vast head. I don't know what
to do about it though. It's very embarrassing to have a
head like that. The veins on my temples are as thick as
ropes; my blood courses through them, pressing against
the bluish walls and making them swell up. And I say
to myself: 'What must everyone be thinking!' I stand in
the half-darkness of the doorway and when I believe
myself unobserved for a moment I am just about to
raise my hands quickly to feel my head . . . But there's
that young man again, though he's on the other side of
the street now. He has his hands in his pockets, and he's

pretending to be bored with having nothing to do; he's whistling a foolish tune of some sort and walking slowly up and down, apparently interested in nothing in particular. But I'm not a fool; I can see quite plainly that he's watching me.

What does the fellow want? I can't help it if suddenly I've got this tremendous head; it embarrasses me too.

He goes on whistling and walking up and down, squinting over at me from time to time. 'The best thing is to take no notice of him,' I think. 'Just pretend you're not interested in anything either.' I step forward out of the doorway so that he can see me better if he wants to, put my hand to my chin as though in thought, look up into the sky, and pretend that I'm completely occupied with myself and my affairs. But all the time I keep my eye on him and I notice that suddenly he starts grinning. Not about my head. No, it's just that he's seen through my little ruse, that's all. And then suddenly I hear his thoughts.

He's thinking: 'You silly old man, do you really think I can't see through you?' At that I retreat once more into the shelter of the doorway. My head is really tremendous now and it's swelling up more and more. It's becoming too heavy for me and I lean against the doorway. The pulse hammers in the blood stream and my forehead tips backward gently. I'm not feeling well now and I close my eyes. Then I hear steps, but I'm too scared to open my eyes again. I listen to the steps and my blood courses quicker. I open my eyes just a little bit, and on the street in front of me I see feet. They are coming towards me, the toes turned up and the soles planting themselves on the pavement with deliberation.

My head feels on fire now, and I can't move. I keep

my eyes fixed on those feet. They come nearer still, creeping towards me, nearer and nearer. I want to shout, to call for help, to defend myself, beat my head against the wall. But I'm as though paralysed. I can't do a thing. The feet have come right up close to me now; they're right below my eyes. I can feel their owner's breath on my face, and suddenly I shout: "What do you want?" The young man is standing in front of me. His face is only a few inches from mine. He grins at me and says: "Give me a little something, please."

I wake up, sweating over my whole body, and still very frightened. I sit up, look around, put my hand over to Claudia—and then suddenly I realize that she's dead. And I think to myself: 'You've been dreaming. Don't let it upset you. Go to sleep again.' I wipe the sweat from my forehead and rub the dream out of my eyes. And then suddenly I notice that my head is perfectly normal in size; neither too big nor too small; just right. That pleases and relieves me. I breathe deeply and then I think: 'Don't be silly! The whole thing's nonsense.' But I don't drop off to sleep any more.

XXXIV

Now that really was a change. But certainly not one I'd like to repeat often.

"An informative chat." Now you mustn't think that's something in which each interlocutor sets himself out to give the other information. Oh no! You question the other fellow, and he questions you, and each keeps his own ideas to himself.

A message came from Cassius to the effect that he would very much like to speak to "his friend Pilate"; and if I felt "the desirability of exchanging ideas of a purely informative character" he would be very pleased.

As a matter of fact, I didn't feel any such desire, but I went all the same.

There are people who have a hunched back, and other people think: 'Pity that a man like that should have a hunched back.' Other people squint, and you ask yourself: "Now why does he of all people have to squint?" And then, of course, some people are just stupid, and you think: 'Well, I suppose he can't help it.'

When you're with Cassius you don't question, think or have an opinion. He is without all originality, and he is beloved of all. When he presents himself to the people he smiles and keeps his hands folded over his belly. Isn't he a splendid fellow? Of course the people don't really know anything about him at all. They don't know, for example, that although he's really rather stupid, he's nevertheless very vain and ambitious. And he's no judge of wine, except that he knows which is strong and makes you drunk quickly, and which isn't and doesn't. (And the preliminary stage of being drunk for him means telling dirty stories and being generally swinish, to be followed at the next stage by bellowing, then incoherent babblings, and finally drunken sleep.) But what does that matter? From time to time he lets it be bruited abroad that he has given a slave so and so much money, that he's in mourning for his favourite dog, or that he spent an hour talking to a shepherd boy, although he had "something better to do".

That's not true, of course: he had nothing better to do. If he didn't make a gift of money, didn't mourn for his dog, didn't stroke the head of a shepherd boy, then what on earth should he do to occupy his time? Of course, he doesn't do these things just for fun; his idea is to make himself popular, and that's all part of his publicity. And it brings him in money, power, fame, reputation and favour. And how else is he to make himself popular if not by making presents of money to slaves, by displaying his fondness for dogs, and by talking condescendingly to children? Who knows outside his circle that he's indifferent to his wife? That he deceives her? That when he's drunk he gets violent? Certainly not the people. Cassius knows his job. His paid agents are always busy all over Rome letting it be known what a splendid and sensible fellow he is. And let anyone try to contradict it!

He is typical of our statesmen. His speeches are not stupid, but that's because he doesn't prepare them himself. The slave secretary who does that has to keep his mouth shut about it. And he does too, because so long as he keeps his mouth shut he's in clover. He's well treated and he earns a lot of money; and, in addition, he can maintain an illicit relationship with the wife of Cassius, and with impunity. Every few months Cassius himself spends a while in a brothel in Sirmio where, according to our faithful reporters of the daily journals, he convalesces and recovers his vigour after the worries and troubles the affairs of the Roman Empire impose on him. And his wife keeps her mouth shut too. She is quite clever enough not to cause her husband any embarrassment. What good would it do her? The Emperor wouldn't like it if she did, and, in any case, no one would believe her. After all, to consort with a whore isn't adultery in the eyes of the law. Of course, she's saddled with a man she doesn't love. But does that matter much? She has money, jewellery, clothing, position, a palace, servants, and a lover on top of all that. What more does she want? And what would she be without him? Just a woman—not a great deal nowadays—and despised, cast out, looked down on with contempt, and perhaps half starved.

So she takes good care to stay what she is, even if she does have to lie. And he stays what he is and lies too. They live their indifferent lives, lie their way from banquet to banquet through the year, are respected and honoured; and when the time comes for them to close their puffy eyes for ever they won't even wonder why their lives had to be like that and not otherwise. If you questioned them on the point they would answer vaguely, "That's life", or something like that. And if you questioned them a little more closely: "Did you see the turn when the thirteen-year-old boy was torn to pieces by the lion?" They'd answer: "Yes. Wasn't he marvellous? We all admired the boy's courage tremendously, and we drank to him afterwards. The Emperor enjoyed it very much too. That evening I wore my big gold bangle for the first time, and got to know F. . . . It was all very beautiful. What's the matter with you?"

The matter with me? Oh, nothing really. I was just a failure as a Governor, but now I'm satisfied if I can lead my life to its end more or less in peace. You're quite right, of course; what's the matter with me? What on earth do I want? More ideas? More headaches? Of course, I know you really think me very stupid because I hadn't the wit to make enough money to see me handsomely through the rest of my life when I was a Governor and had the chance. Behind my back you say to each other: "For years on end Pilate had plenty of opportunity to feather his nest. He was right at the source. He only had to stretch out his hand; and he was too stupid to use his chances."

No, I wasn't stupid. It's just that I thought differently about such matters. I thought: if you don't exploit your position of trust to make money for yourself, if you don't play ducks and drakes with your responsibilities, then you will make a good Governor and have every likelihood of being in office for a long time.

To-day I know better, of course. Steal, rob, plunder, enrich yourself! Exploit them to the top of your bent! That's exactly the right thing to do, because who dares to oppose a man who steals, robs, plunders and enriches himself shamelessly? The more audacious you are the more uncertain your enemies become. That's nothing to do with courage. You have to have more courage to sustain the role of a dismissed Governor than you do that of a Cassius in favour. To be regarded as a charlatan without being a charlatan, now that's something; to function as an Emperor without being an Emperor, that's a state. The insane laugh of a lunatic on the freak market does more to change the world than a household run with four hundred slaves; and whoever sits down because he has nothing better to do and starts thinking, does more than the zealous nitwit who sows enemies of the State. A State always has enemies, and it does the right thing if it encourages them, because if it persecutes them they will make common cause and soon become a real power.

But I'm quite calm all the same. It's night, Rome is just as deaf as my ears. It's raining. And I'm alone again.

Although I expressly ordered Eleazar to give up his nightly extravagances and to drop all this nonsense with the Christians, he's out of the house again. His audacity astonishes me. He knew that I should be back late and that I would notice that he had left the house. And yet he went. Of course, he knows that I'm helpless nowadays and that I shan't strike him; and on that account alone I'm in the wrong as far as he's concerned. Slaves need to be beaten. He also knows that it's very unlikely that I shall turn him out. I've got much too used to him for that. Who's right now? I or my slave?

But I won't put up with it all the same. Whether it's clever of me or not I'll get rid of him.

On the other hand, I can understand this urge people feel to believe in a Messiah. They don't know any more what they are to believe in. Whoever believes in the gods falls sick, becomes poor, is ridiculed, loses his job, is demoted, and regarded as stupid. And whatever he does he has a bad conscience; he tries to be decent, and yet he's always tripping up; he's afraid of treachery, corruption, lies and swindling; he doesn't commit adultery (and his wife regards that as mere weakness); people call him a hypocrite, a fanatic, old-fashioned. And people laugh at him, because the world's going to the dogs anyway, and it really won't matter much then whether a man was well in with the gods or not. People feel sorry for him because he's so naïve as to take the gods seriously; because he makes his own life a misery, failing to see that the greatest god is the Emperor (a god with a very loose tongue incidentally). And even when he's quite determined to take all that on his shoulders some temple servant comes along and tells him that he's all wrong anyway; so he just doesn't know what to think any more.

The cleverer ones have already found themselves new gods. They believe in the Emperor, in the heroes of the circus, in the fashionable actors and the successful advocates. They're fast-living gods.

Others just dismiss the gods altogether. It's all a swindle anyway, they say; and they devote themselves zealously to piling up the sesterces.

But actually the best thing to do is to pile up the sesterces whilst outwardly believing in the gods. The more money you make the more you bend your spine in public in honour of the gods. That's the safest thing to do.

But they're all swine!

The result is this Messiah mania.

Of course, perhaps that's all a bit over-simplified. We must try our best to get ourselves out of the mire. But we're too contemptible for that.

It's odd that the discussion with Cassius no longer upsets me. I was hardly in his house when he handed me the three missing pages of notes, saying:

"You must be more careful, Pilate."

I didn't know what he was getting at, and I took the pages, looked at them, recognized my handwriting, and asked:

"What is this?"

"Didn't you write it?"

I considered the matter for a moment or two, but it would have been quite senseless to attempt to deceive him.

"Yes," I said. "They're notes of mine."

"Well, in that case take them and look after them a bit better."

I put them away. I couldn't remember what there was

in those notes, but I felt that the situation was more than just dangerous.

"Do you trust me now?" asked Cassius.

"What do you mean 'now'? Have I ever mistrusted you?"

"No, of course not; that's not what I wanted to say. Understand me rightly: I merely wanted to provide you with some earnest of my reliability."

('Provide?' That's an odd word, I thought.)

"Just a little gesture, nothing more," he went on. "It's just that I'd like you to be quite sure that I am well disposed towards you, Pilate. That's all."

'Which way's the cat going to jump?' I thought. I realized that he wanted something from me, but what I couldn't imagine.

"You got those pages from Stephanio, of course," I said calmly.

"How do you mean?"

"What is there to mean? Just that you got those pages from Stephanio. Isn't that so?"

"What makes you think that?"

"Oh, just one of those things."

He fell silent and that was enough for me. Then he raised his glass and drank to me. After which he moved closer to me and began to talk urgently. His voice was so low that I had some difficulty in understanding him at all. His lips were full and fleshy and smooth with spittle. I tried to read what he was saying from them, but it's difficult to read lips like that. But I did understand that he was asking me whether I knew that Stephanio was a secret agent.

Of course I didn't know it. I never give even a thought to such things, such occupations just don't exist for me.

But I told him that I had already heard a rumour to that effect; someone had already warned me against him.

At that Cassius looked at me a trifle doubtfully, and then drank to me again. After that he put on his most important mien and advised me to be careful of Stephanio. He, Cassius, was well disposed towards me, he repeated. I must know that, he said. And it hurt him to see a man like me cast to one side, in disfavour with the Emperor, and spied on by secret agents. Of course, he went on, it was quite possible that he himself had the reputation of being a staunch supporter of the Emperor, but in his heart of hearts he was really quite different; he could assure me of that. He was a friend of all free spirits, a friend of truth and of frankness. But in his position he had no alternative. We were all living dangerously. And those who were apparently powerful were in even greater danger than those who merely strung along. Incidentally, I could have no real idea of what he had to put up with. No one could really. His position was not enviable. In his heart of hearts he was with the poor and the oppressed, but what could he do? After all, he was only a small link in the chain, a cog-wheel in the machinery, nothing more. If, on the other hand, he really had an opportunity to rule, then things would be very different; I could be sure of that.

He looked at me and I nodded. I didn't believe a word he said, but I nodded. Then he went on:

If things did happen to change, what side would I be on? Could he rely on me? He did not wish to offend me; and, of course, he knew that I was always on the side of justice. Oh yes, he knew that very well, but in days like these one just had to make quite certain of one's supporters in advance.

He drank my health again.

'Is he planning a *coup d'état*?' I wondered. 'But, no, rebels are made of very different stuff. I've had some experience of them. But in that case, what *is* he after?'

I then told him that I didn't think I'd altogether understood him—on account of my deafness, I said in my excuse; and I asked him to set down briefly and clearly what he wanted. And I handed him my writing materials.

That was perfidious of me, of course. I knew perfectly well that he wouldn't give me a single word in writing. People like Cassius will stand by nothing the moment it suits them not to, so, naturally, they don't want anything in writing. They pay with sesterces, and the other fellow carries his skin to the market place. From one minute to the next Cassius and his like can say the exact opposite of what they said before, and they're so slippery that no one can prove a thing against them.

He treated my request jokingly; drank to me again, laughed, poured some more out for me, and then said that he and I didn't need anything in writing. Friends could trust each other's word. I should therefore put away my writing materials.

I did, and I knew already that I had made myself a new and powerful enemy. Cassius had not given me back my notes for nothing. . . . For him and his like nothing is for nothing.

Then he clapped his hands, and some girls came in and danced. They were naked under transparent draperies. Boys sang. Cassius became merry, made jokes, and called out something or other to the girls. My eyes were fixed on them eagerly; the flesh, the music. My eyes stared, sought a hold. I drank, pretending to be bored, and looked at them again. Boys, wine, girls! Cassius laughed, slapped his thigh and took one of the girls. I drank. The girls, their dancing, the bodies of the boys, the wine, the tipsiness, the flesh. 'Nothing matters now,' I thought. 'They're dancing. You're here. That's life; you can't change it. That girl there is beautiful. She's smiling at you; she doesn't care that you're not Governor of Judea any more. Drink! You've got your notes back, and there's the girl, her willing arms, her breasts . . .'

Then I remembered Claudia. I had a headache, and I got up and said good-bye.

"You're going already?" said Cassius in surprise.

"Yes," I said. "I'm going now."

"As you please."

He obviously didn't understand me. But there, I didn't understand myself either.

Stephanio a secret agent? He borrows money from me he never pays back, and at the same time he spies on me. He abuses the Emperor in order to trick me into abusing him too. And if I had fallen into his trap he would have gone to his superiors, whoever they are, and reported: "Mission executed", and held out his hand for his reward. And they'd have paid him his money. But what should I do when this creature visited me again, as no doubt he would before long?

Ask after his health? And then what? Which didn't solve the problem of what Cassius wanted from me. I wasn't quite sure myself. It was light outside. The milkmen were loudly crying their wares. A group of schoolchildren were disputing noisily. I wonder what they learn in school these days? Reading, writing, and now and again a poem. And the more they learn of that sort of thing the less capable they will be of living their lives subsequently. That's how it goes.

But what did Cassius want? Who knows? Perhaps all he wanted was to relieve his conscience of a burden. Perhaps he thinks: 'Pilate is an honest man who has been the victim of injustice. Not much I can do about it, of course, but I'll invite him to spend an evening with me; chat to him, give him plenty to drink, and offer him naked girls.'

And now he's done it his conscience is clear again.

It would be a good idea to hire out such a conscience as that by the hour.

I've been lying down for a good hour but I can't go to sleep. It's light and there's a lot of noise on the street. Not that I can hear it; the noise bores into the head nerves. I was thinking of calling Eleazar and asking him what he thinks of Stephanio, but in the end I didn't: I shouldn't get a frank answer anyway.

Well, and what now?

That's an important question. Or is it? You limp from happening to happening, and make up your mind to draw the consequences, but whatever you do you just limp along.

One ought to treat the dead as though they were alive; and the living as though they were dead. Then I should only have loved Claudia.

By the way, Cassius said I was a good Roman. A good Roman? What do I care about Rome? What do I care about the great Roman Empire? Am I supposed to love it? What for? Our beautiful language? People go to sleep if you ask them to listen to a recitation of an ode by Horace. Our culture? It's being done to death by people like Cassius and his friends. Me a good Roman? Anything but! Just someone who's still alive and is called Pilate.

Someone who becomes a caricature as soon as you take him seriously.

But who isn't a caricature as soon as you take him seriously?

Let me concentrate.

Let us suppose a hundred people were brought together and told to agree on the question of what a human being is. On the understanding that if they can't agree they'll be put into prison and kept there until they do. They might, for example, come to the conclusion that a human being was a creature which thinks.

Good!

And one of them would then say: human beings have advocates, offices, beggars, secret police, Christianity, lodging houses, night-watchmen, sensation-hunters, gladiatorial combats, brothels, artificial egg-hatching, elephant deaths, pseudo-marriages, executions by adder bite, naked actresses, jokes, usurers, brokers, wonders, dice games, parasites, tame parrots, popular-song hits, animal tamers, world-peace fanatics, gods, and so on.

How does that fit into their definition?

It doesn't, so they have to come together again and think of a new formula. Without success. It's impossible. They'd never find one. All they'd find was that I'm a bit off my head.

And what about you?

Oh, sorry!

It's raining cats and dogs. A man hurries by shaking himself like a dog. There seems no one at home in the house of Cassius across the way. Everything seems empty, dead and silent. Of course, that's only what it looks like. In reality Cassius is still snoring. His wife has her lover with her. And somewhere or other a slave is counting money.

Aren't I ever going to get to sleep?

I'm trying, but it's difficult.

XXXV

I'VE dismissed Eleazar.

He took it very calmly.

Because his behaviour offended me, I said. "You don't seem very upset about it," I added.

"Oh, indeed, master."

"Well, then . . ."

"Thy will be done, master."

There you have it! A slave hardly cares who his master is. One's as good as another. But the master gets used to his slave. Turn it the other way round and it fits again.

"Do you know why I'm dismissing you?"

"Yes."

"Why, then?"

"Because I'm a Christian."

"No, that's not true; you can be what you like. I don't care. It's just that I don't want you to leave the house at night."

"To whom are you going to sell me, master?"

"Sell yourself. Do what you like."

At that he wept, and then unfortunately I felt sorry for him, so I said:

"Write down for me what it is you expect to find with the Christians, and then we'll see."

Very well, I got my answer. Here it is:

"Master,

"I have become a Christian. There are no gods; there is only one God.

"This God is a God of mercy. We are all equal in his sight. He does not mind whether we are Emperor or slave. He minds only whether we have a kind heart. I want to have a kind heart. God's son died for us because we are all bad. We are loaded with sins, and through his death God's son takes our sins from us.

"I love you, master, but I love God more. He is my first master.

"If you compel me to choose between Him and you, then I must choose Him.

"Please do not be angry with me, master.

(Sig.) Eleazar"[1]

I've nothing to say to that. Except that it doesn't really matter what a man believes. Even this State has the one virtue of being tolerant in matters of religious belief. To-day you can believe anything or nothing, just as the fancy takes you. Nobody minds. But what Eleazar says undermines the idea of the State, and that makes it dangerous. But what does it matter to me?

[1] The original of this document is missing. There is only the copy available.   L.P.B.

XXXVI

FURTHER discussion with Barabbas:

"You wanted a Messiah; is that right?"

"Yes, it is."

"He was going to free you; is that right?"

"Yes."

"What exactly was he going to free you from?"

"From all force and violence."

"Does that mean he's an enemy of Rome then?"

"No, it doesn't."

"What does it mean then?"

"It means that his kingdom is not of this world."

"I see, not of this world. Which world then?"

"He died for us on the cross."

"That's interesting, but for the moment it's not to the point. Your zealotry to one side if you don't mind. Let's get down to facts. We're not chatting together for our amusement, you know. I want to get at the truth, and the truth as far as it interests me is tangible and to the point. Do you understand that?"

"I used to think I understood it at one time, but he has nothing to do with politics."

"That's right enough. He was a harmless creature who didn't understand the scrape he had got himself into. I was sorry for him. I didn't want his life; it was his own people who demanded that of me."

"But you ordered his execution."

"True, but I opposed it as long as I could. You know that."

"Yes, I know that."

"What should it have mattered to me that the High Priests wanted to see a Jesus, a Moses or a Judas on the cross?"

"Not a Moses or a Judas perhaps, but a Jesus."

"Why?"

"Because you probably noticed something."

"What should I have noticed?"

"That he was the Messiah."

"But I was exclusively interested in the political side of the affair. The Messiah was to rouse you to rebellion. That's right, isn't it?"

"He wanted the truth."

"Truth! What is truth? Truth for you is that the Romans must disappear from Judea. For me it is that they must stay. Another truth is that you're alive and Jesus is dead. And truth again is that I am asking the questions and you have to answer them. Have you got that into your head?"

"He died for me on the cross."

"Don't waste time; that's what I said: for you. That's your truth. But why should it be mine?"

"You didn't know him, sir."

"On the contrary, I knew him quite well. He was a poor innocent wretch who had no idea of the danger he had got himself into."

"You didn't see him die."

"No, I didn't see him die. But I've seen a good few people die in my time and one gets used to it. It's much the same."

"Not with him."

139

"Don't you feel yourself that you're gradually getting a bit silly? All right, so he died for you. I know he did. You had a stroke of luck. But why should a fellow like you make such a fuss about it? It isn't in keeping at all."

"I'm not making a fuss about it; I'm just saying what is."

"What is! The truth, in other words? Isn't that right?"

"Yes."

"Very well, the truth. Will you now tell me how you recognize the truth when you see it?"

"You didn't see him."

"I didn't see him? Of course I saw him. You know I saw him. I also spoke to him. I knew that he hadn't harmed a fly. Your precious High Priests played him into my hands against my will. They used every possible legalistic trick; they coaxed and persuaded and wheedled; they even threatened, and they almost blackmailed me, in order to make me order his crucifixion. That's the truth, my truth."

Barabbas said nothing.

"You may think differently on the point, but there, you have a bad conscience. You think to yourself: 'Actually I ought to have hung on the cross, but he took my place.' And that's upset you a bit; but only because you're not really a strong man after all, but a weakling."

"He died for me on the cross."

"That's gradually being borne in on me."

"But not only for me."

"Not only for you? For whom else then?"

"For everyone, for all of us."

"Very interesting. Does that include me?"

"It includes all of us."

"But I didn't remotely come into the question."

Barabbas was silent.

"I said that I didn't come into the question at all. There was no cross erected for me."

"No, of course not."

"Well, what have you got to say then?"

"He was the son of God."

"You don't say so!"

"Yes, he truly was."

"Yes, really and truly. I know the expression."

"Believe me, sir."

"Why should I believe you?"

"Because what I say is the truth."

"So we've come round to the truth again. Well, as I asked before without getting a satisfactory answer: what is truth?"

"You didn't see him die."

"No, I didn't. But one thing strikes me: you seem to have gone up in the world a bit. God personally allowed his own son to be crucified in order to lengthen your worthless life. Well, that's a fine thing, I must say! Are you related to him by any chance? You must have good connections. Or is this god a rich uncle of yours?"

"Your mockery does not hurt me."

"But your arrogance is insulting to me."

Barabbas remained silent.

"Did you understand me?"

"Yes, I understood you."

"Very well, answer."

"There is nothing to say."

"Very well, let's get down to simple facts. This Messiah of yours is a Freedom Hero, a nationalist prophet; is that right?"

"Many think so."

"What is it exactly they think?"

"They think a Messiah will come who will free Israel and drive the Romans out of the country."

"Ah, now we're coming to something! I understand that. That is a reality, a dangerous one certainly, but at least tangible. And *that's* the Messiah I have to deal with. I don't believe in him, of course, but I recognize him as a power. And I am in charge of the Roman occupation forces. Is that clear?"

"Yes, that's perfectly clear."

"Now the people expect miracles of him; is that right?"

"Perfectly right."

"They expect power, strength and glory?"

"Yes."

"What's he supposed to look like?"

"There is no detailed description available."

"Do your people still believe in a Messiah?"

"Yes, they do."

"But you tell me he's dead; that he died for you. How does that fit in?"

"They didn't recognize him."

"But you recognized him all right?"

"Yes, I did."

"Have you special eyes or something then?"

"No, but he performed miracles."

"Which were disproved according to the High Priests. But we needn't discuss that. I am the jurist here, not you."

"His miracles were subject to no law."

"How did he manage that?"

"Because he was the son of God."

"Yes, yes, you've already said that. And you and a

few others recognized him as the son of God, but all the others were blind or foolish. That's what you mean, isn't it?"

"You don't understand me, sir."

"I think I do. Very well indeed, in fact. You and your friends have swallowed this Jesus business hook, line and sinker, and now you think you're something better than the others; you're privileged persons. Do you understand what I mean?"

"Yes, I understand perfectly."

"And can you perhaps see now that this Messiah hope of the people is a dangerous business?"

"Dangerous for whom?"

"For you, for your country, and for your lives."

"A danger for Rome perhaps, if my people rise. But there will be no second Messiah. Never."

XXXVII

ONE day my men brought a prisoner before me. They believed him to be a spy. He admitted being a Freedom Fighter, was very proud of it in fact; babbled the usual nationalistic phrases; talked ecstatically about the Messiah and his rule—but in the end it turned out that the fellow wasn't quite right in the head. He mixed up everything in a really senseless fashion. I ordered him to be released.

Afterwards my men had a bit of fun with him. A captain said to him solemnly: "Listen, last night I dreamt of this Messiah. Do you know that in my dream he looked very much like you?"

The poor wretch grinned, and the soldiers laughed.

"Really," the captain went on. "I'm being quite serious. You're exactly like the Messiah I saw in my dream."

"Is that really true," the half-wit demanded.

"As true as I'm standing here."

Now the soldiers caught on, and they began to shout: "Long live the Messiah!" "The Messiah has been sent to us!", and they crowded round the young fellow, drank to him, saluted him solemnly, and behind his back they laughed uproariously at their little joke.

But the young half-wit took it all very seriously.

"Do you really think I look like the Messiah?" he asked the jocular captain.

"Absolutely," the captain assured him.

"Long live the Messiah!" the soldiers shouted. "Three cheers for the Messiah!"

"I'll tell you something then," the young fellow went on seriously. "I too had a dream, and in it I heard a voice say: 'You are to be the Messiah!' And now when you tell me the same thing . . ."

"Well, if you had a dream like that too," said the captain, "I can't think what you're waiting for. You're obviously the Messiah, beyond all possible doubt."

At this the soldiers roared again: "Unto us a Messiah is given!" "Long live the Messiah!" "Fetch wine! Give him to drink! We'll all get drunk on it!"

"Oh no," said the young man, "if I'm the Messiah I mustn't drink any more. I'll go through the land telling everyone I'm the Messiah."

The soldiers laughed, shouted and drank.

"Right, then! Off you go!" "Long live the new Messiah!" "Drink to the health of the new prophet!" And they made up a drinking song on the spur of the moment:

"We've seen the Messiah!
"Hurrah, hurrah, hurrah!
"He'll bring us lots of fun,
"And we'll drink another one!
"We've seen the Messiah!
"Hurrah, hurrah, hurrah!"

The young half-wit was delighted with his new role, and he bowed a little clumsily to left and right, and waved to everyone. The soldiers were doubled up with laughter, and they slapped their thighs, drank deep draughts and had a great deal of fun out of the poor fellow, who now turned to the captain and announced:

"And you will go with me through the land, because it was through you that God gave me the sign."

"Oh, splendid," exclaimed the captain. "When do we start?"

"At once. There's no time to lose. The people must know immediately."

"But I can't go at once. I've got to pack my things."

"There's no time for that. God has called you and you must follow me."

"And supposing I refuse?"

"But I order you to."

At that the captain could no longer remain serious and he burst out laughing. But the half-wit was offended at such frivolity and began to threaten.

"If you laugh at me I will strike you dumb. Now follow me at once."

The soldiers began to sing their song again, adding a

few topical verses to it about their captain and his journey with the new Messiah through the land.

The Messiah fell silent for a while; apparently he was thinking the matter over.

"You're silent, Messiah," someone said. "Are you talking to God?"

"You must not disturb me," the young fellow said grandly.

"Of course not! Who'd dare to do such a thing? But I'll tell you what we'll do: we'll all kick you up the bum to help you on your way through the land."

At that there was a roar of approval from the soldiers but the "Messiah" remained calm, and turning to the captain he asked:

"If I am the Messiah what shall I say to the people?"

"Oh, just tell them you will cast down the walls of Jerusalem. And when they see them lying in ruins they'll know you really are the Messiah."

But the captain and his men were getting a bit tired of the joke now; it was going on too long, so they drove the young half-wit away.

During the next three days thirty thousand people came into Jerusalem because they had heard that a new Messiah had appeared and said that he would destroy the walls of Jerusalem, and everyone should come and look at them for himself and be convinced.

Thirty thousand people flocking into Jerusalem on account of a young half-wit and the ribaldry of a group of soldiers!

But such jokes have their obverse side too. For example the bandits knew that they could continue to exist only so long as the people believed in the coming of a Messiah, so they sent out false prophets in order that the Messianic idea should not be forgotten amongst the people. Almost every week bandits disguised as respectable citizens would walk through the streets of Jerusalem assuring the people that God would send them a Messiah in the near future. And that all they needed was patience.

When it came to the point they were ice cold and utterly ruthless; and neither God nor any other means were too base for them. Though sometimes they were themselves caught up in the illusion, like Barabbas; though that didn't happen often.

XXXVIII

Now they were three weeks I shan't forget in a hurry! Actually I suppose I ought to be glad that I'm still alive. But am I?

They searched the whole place and turned almost everything upside down. But they didn't find anything. Actually my notes were lying openly on the table in the middle of the room together with one or two maxims of Socrates, and one or two of Eleazar's messages. But, of course, people like that don't look for things which are just on a table top; it's secret hiding-places they're after! So they look under the floor, behind the walls and in the garden. They tell themselves that what an enemy of the State does not bother to conceal can be of no interest to them. Their logic must have gone something like this: Pilate is an enemy of the Emperor, an enemy of the State, an enemy of the people; quite clearly therefore he must have some secret hiding-place where he conceals his plans. The idea that I might leave my notes clearly visible on the table just didn't occur to them; they'd much sooner dig up the garden looking for secret chests.

During the examination they struck me. I don't know who they were; such people are always anonymous. I pretended to be even deafer than I was; tried, in fact, to persuade them that I was as deaf as a post and couldn't hear a thing. But all my scheming as to the best way to conduct myself led to nothing in the end. So finally I thought only of Claudia. I love her.

Sometimes I thought: 'If you only had someone *now*, someone who would take you by the hand and say: "Don't worry, I'm here with you." '

But there was no one with me—unless you count someone who punches you in the face and says: "Come on now, what about it?"

But apart from that I was alone.

No one to pat me on the shoulder and say: "Good luck!"

No one at all.

Not even someone with a headache to whom you could say: "Yes, I know just what that feels like."

They don't have headaches. They just couldn't pat anyone on the back amiably. All they can do with their hands is to double them into fists and punch you in the face. And they kick you too, in the behind. Most humiliating—and painful too. Their eyes are either half asleep or gleaming with hate. Their tongues shout abuse, or indulge in swinishness. They would sooner beat a man to death than give him a glass of water. But you get used to people like that too.

I have come to the conclusion that my conscience sits somewhere between my eyes and the place where those headaches start, because that's more or less where it hurts when I do anything which violates my conscience. There isn't any spot that hurts *them*. They don't even see what's right before their eyes; they see only what they want to see. "Headaches?" they ask. "What's that? You don't mean to tell me that enemies of the State have headaches?"

Naturally I made no answer to such questions. Pleading deafness, I pretended not to have heard them at all.

After ten days they got an idea: as I couldn't hear what they said, or couldn't be persuaded to hear what they said, why not communicate with me in writing? It took them some time to get round to this simple solution, but in the end they did.

They drew up a questionnaire for me to fill in. Here it is:

1. What do you think of the Emperor?

"*Not much*" would have been my honest answer, but instead I wrote:

"The Emperor is a great man. He thinks for us all. Whatever should we do if he didn't think for us any more? It's unimaginable."

2. What do you think is wrong with the State?

I ought to have written:

Almost everything. The worst thing about it, I think, is that it pretends that everyone has the right to think for himself and say what he thinks, but actually it crushes everyone who dares to think for himself and say what he thinks. But what I actually wrote was:

"Our State is very good indeed. It is guided by honourable and upright men; and honourable and upright men are in its service. If I might dare to make a suggestion it is more out of frankness than wisdom.

"It is just that more comfort stations should be erected in one or two squares in the city. But on more mature consideration they are probably quite unnecessary."

3. What is your attitude to the gods?

Thanks for the question. I'm on perfectly good terms with them. I don't believe in them at all, but that really doesn't matter.

Actual answer: "In that respect I gratefully follow the example of the Emperor himself, who is my model. If he decided to abolish the gods I should be completely on his side. But seeing that the gods love the Emperor he will hardly wish to abolish them. And that's a very good thing."

4. Do you believe in the world power of Rome, or in the often prophesied end of the world?

I have a bruise in the middle of my back about the size of a small plate. It witnesses the zeal of a loyal servant of the Emperor. I believe in that. I just have to believe in that, because the moment I try to lie on my back it gives me a great deal of pain.

But what I actually wrote was:

"Of course I believe in Rome. In the ordinary way I should regard it as beneath my dignity to deign to answer such a question, but as I know that it has been put by honourable men, I do reply."

5. What do you think of secret agents?

Bit perfidious that question, isn't it? A scoundrel like Stephanio endangers my life for the sake of a few wretched sesterces, and now I'm expected to write him an honourable recommendation!

I actually wrote:

"Secret agents are most necessary and useful creatures. They keep their eyes open to see that nothing happens in the State that ought not to happen. Seeing that nothing ought to happen which ought not to happen, secret agents are therefore necessary and useful."

6. What do you have to say to the charge that in the depths of your heart you are an enemy of the State?

What can I say? First of all nothing at all. But then, and from the depths of my heart, I will say: if this State pays any attention to malicious rumour-mongers whilst at the same time causing the tenets of Socrates to be taught in its schools, then this State is a living lie.

But I wrote:

"I am an honest man, but, of course, I can make a mistake like anyone else. But where I do make a mistake I will never cease to regret it."

7. Can you prove that what you have to say is the truth?

No, of course I can't, silly; because in the first place I'm lying; and in the second place it's very difficult to prove the truth. It proves itself.

But I wrote:

"My whole behaviour proves it."

What shall I do with my notes now? Hide them? Or destroy them? But I think if I burnt them they would be far more likely to find a few fatal if charred words in the ashes than they would if I just left them on the table.

In the meantime, because of the bruises on my back, I have to sleep on my belly for the Empire. And if I sleep worse on that account then that only goes to show that I'm a pretty low type.

XXXIX

I'VE been asking myself whether my answers to that questionnaire were cowardly. They were utterly dishonest, of course, that's quite clear. But they weren't made any braver by their ironic undertone. I knew perfectly well that those loyal servants of the Emperor wouldn't even smell irony. They take just everything at its face value; if the Emperor promoted himself to be a god it would be perfectly all right with them. Which doesn't alter the fact that I'm a coward.[1]

On the other hand, if that is so then courage would mean that one has to be honest even towards the most savage brute—even in the knowledge that he will immediately reward you for your pains by maiming or killing you. Should I really go in for self-mutilation?

Whilst I was away Eleazar kept everything in perfect order. They questioned him too, of course, but he "knew nothing", and that seemed likely. After all, he is a slave. Claudia's room untouched. When I came back he kissed my hands.

In this somewhat embarrassing fashion a slave forces his master to be loyal to him.

[1] I began to find it more and more difficult not to censor the increasingly shameful utterances of the former Governor of Judea. But although they fill my heart with loathing, I propose to assume, rightly I hope, and with humble respect, that it is not my responsibility to destroy them. My decision is also affected by the consideration that it is highly probable that by this time the former Governor of Judea was already suffering from advanced senile decay.   L.P.B.

XL

Claudia:

A CAT has adopted me. It's rather an ugly cat really, with wretched stumps of teeth, and a dirty pelt, bare in patches.

I've decided to keep it.

She keeps out of my way, but when we meet she looks at me with her penetrating, impenetrable eyes; and makes me wonder what she's thinking about me. Nothing to my advantage I take it. However, I've very good reason to know how mistaken you can be with that sort of snap judgement. For example, Stephanio's eyes look as though they could weep with compassion at a moment's notice. A most compassionate man, you might suppose.

The cat stands there and looks at me. "No," I say to myself, "you're not an actor, and you're also not a secret agent. You're just a nice cat, soft and friendly, with a warm coat. . . ."

I go to pick her up, to take her in my lap and stroke her, but she has other ideas and she walks away.

'You could give her something to eat,' I think. 'If you did she'd probably come back again.'

"There you are," I say to her a bit later, "I've brought you something to eat."

But she didn't let herself be won that way. She hid herself somewhere; perhaps behind the heating. I go down on my knees, put my head down to floor level and look for her, making encouraging noises for her benefit. But she's got a will of her own.

I can't see her body, only her eyes. They're narrow and green. They're staring at me and coldly glistening, looking through and through me. I wonder what her eyes are thinking.

They're thinking: 'Here we are glistening and staring at you. And when you go away I'll wait for a while until I can't see you, hear you, or smell you any more; and then I'll come out to see what you've brought me to eat.'

But I remain kneeling with my head at floor level, and continue encouragingly: "Puss, puss, puss!" But it has no effect whatever. 'She doesn't like you,' I think. 'Do something else.' But what?

I get up, look around for something to do, sit down, write a few lines; get up and go out of the room altogether. Come back, write another few lines. Think things over and wait. The cat doesn't move. 'I'm not to be caught as easily as that,' she thinks. She's obviously got all the time in the world.

I get down on the floor again and look into her eyes. Say something and push the plate with the food towards her.

"There you are, pussy! You must be hungry."

Maybe she is hungry, but that doesn't make any difference; she'll eat when she decides to eat, not when I want her to. 'You can wait a long time,' she thinks. 'You can lie there on the floor for six weeks and look at me, and I still won't eat; not even if it kills me.'

'I could go for a walk in the meantime,' I think, and I put on my outdoor clothes and leave the house. On the street there are people, faces, houses, a strange cat and a

crying child. I'm not interested in any of it. I'm thinking:
'What will she do whilst you're away?'

That's easy; she's eaten the food. And disappeared. I
call her, look for her, search through the house calling
her: "Puss, puss, puss." And even "Claudia!"

I can't find her, but I'm going to keep her.

XLI

CASSIUS is dead.

What did he die of?

The doctors just don't know, or say they don't. The
Emperor is deeply moved, of course; and the people are
shattered. His wife weeps, his slaves weep, his little whores
weep—even his relatives let a decent tear or two fall.

'Actually you ought to squeeze out a tear yourself.'
I think. 'It's only decent; after all, the man's dead.'
Then I think of Claudia, and I don't have to squeeze out
any tears.

XLII

OBVERSE of a State:

Who isn't capable of anything else can at least make
money nowadays.

Whoever wants to keep a pure heart must find himself

a place apart. With a pure heart he might, for example, keep chicken, or fill out forms; but he can't be a Senator.

You can keep chicken for two reasons: because you like chicken or out of irony. As the love of chicken depends on egg-laying, and as irony is becoming less and less understood, chicken are gradually dying out.

Socrates died serenely and cheerfully. To-day everything—from ruling to whoring—is done cheerfully and serenely—except dying.

You must be able to prove what you believe, and believe what can be proved. For example, it can readily be proved that Cassius was a great man.

How? quite simple: because at his funeral there were secret agents present to check the jewellery of the women mourners.

Your head is there to think with; your feet to walk with. To-day people walk with their heads and think with their feet: with the left foot hesitant and cowardly, with the right foot in someone's spine.

"I have always acted with the best of intentions."

"Go and string yourself up!"

The Jews hoped for a Messiah.

They were silly enough to believe in it.

We believe far too devoutly to be so stupid.

XLIII

FOR days now Eleazar has been pestering me to go with him to a meeting of the Christians. His enthusiasm astonishes me. I wonder if he's getting paid for it. Or has he perhaps some special interest of his own? As far as I know, most Christians are a very questionable lot. They haven't, for example, the faintest idea of philosophy. However, they're not so dangerous as the Jews, because they regard themselves as a sect, and not as a nation. Their public requirements are modest; at least, so it would seem. According to Eleazar, they teach that all men are equal. That's ridiculous, of course. For example, I'm better than Stephanio both in my desires and in my behaviour.

(Incidentally, I wonder what Stephanio's doing now. Is he still in Rome? Has he another victim to spy on?)

Clothes make the man still. A mob of half-educated people wander around in the garb of philosophers. They dress like Socrates or Diogenes, but apart from the modest ability to write Greek they have nothing but the insolence to be arrogant. They may be quite clever rhetoricians, but they're as far removed from wisdom as Jupiter is from marital faithfulness, or Mercury from probity. The alleged philosophers have brought philosophy into discredit. The common people see a man with a long cloak and long hair and assume that he must be a philosopher; and as soon as he misbehaves himself they declare with satisfaction: "Now look at that! See what he's doing! That isn't the way he talks!"

The false philosophers do a lot of harm. They teach contempt for money, yet give their lessons only for hard cash. They insist that fame is contemptible, but personally they are as vain as peacocks. They tell us that philosophy makes a man passionless, but when they squabble amongst themselves they snap more fiercely than dogs with the rabies. They preach heroism, civil courage and decency, but they flatter every parvenu with money. Quite generally, they're as uncouth as apes, as cowardly as chicken, and as quarrelsome as cocks on a dungheap.

Epilogue

Was with Claudia. Cold, empty and grey. On a tomb-stone I read an inscription:

"He started small and became big—He left thirty million sesterces and never listened to a Philosopher in his life!"

Quod erat demonstrandum.

XLIV

THERE are rumours that Cassius did not die a natural death. As his funeral was very magnificent these rumours are more likely to be true than false.

So far my property has not been confiscated. I reckoned with it after my interrogation. But on consideration I understand why it was not confiscated. They wouldn't like to have to admit that they had treated me badly. If you say to them: "Pilate was recalled, wasn't he?" They will answer: "Recalled? Well, I wouldn't put it that way exactly. Pilate did his duty, of course. He is an honourable man to whom we owe a great deal. But it became necessary to appoint a new Governor, so, of course, we had to do the right thing."

And then if you go on: "But Pilate was spied on?" they will answer: "Spied on? Well, I wouldn't put it that way exactly. You see, just because we think a lot of him we had him watched. We do that with every important person, you know. Even the Emperor himself is closely watched. And if the former Governor is one of those who are still honoured in that way, well, he's to be congratulated, I assure you."

"But," you continue, "they subjected him to an interrogation, and he was beaten."

"Beaten, did you say? Tell me at once the name of the man who struck him so that he can be called to account. Pilate was actually beaten, you say? If that should turn out to be true it would be monstrous. We should have to take good care that the Emperor never hears of it, for if he did, what do you think would happen to the man responsible? He would be banished. No, he would be stoned. You can be quite certain of that."

But, of course, the Emperor will never hear of it. They'll take good care of that. And should he nevertheless somehow hear of it, he'll take good care to take no notice.

"But what's the matter with Pilate? He's been put on the shelf. He's just going to seed. Isn't he any use any more then?"

And the answer will come pat:

"I don't know what you're driving at, really. Why do you make such a fuss about Pilate? Hasn't he everything he needs to live comfortably? Has the State ever been unjust to him? Pilate is respected and honoured. He has his property, and his house, and he lives a quiet, retired life. You wouldn't be attacking the State, by any chance would you?"

Oh no, of course not! For one very good reason if for no other—namely, that no one wants to die. And so you see how it is that they don't take my money away. Pilate mustn't be allowed to perish in misery. No one is to be able to say that.

XLV

LOOKED for my cat.
   Eleazar missing for a couple of hours.
   Hardly ate anything.
   Tried to read. Fell asleep over it.
   Headache.
   Another day got through somehow.

XLVI

ELEAZAR is full of nothing but this Jesus fellow. According to him Jesus is the only begotten son of God. Yet he allowed himself to be nailed to the cross of his own free will, and because that was so he was naturally unable to defend himself. Now he sits at the right hand of God the Father, in Heaven.

I can't say I blame them. After all, they're not fools. They've got eyes in their heads, and they can see what's happening in the world. And because the gods, in whom they hardly believe any longer anyway, don't behave themselves particularly well, going in for adultery, stealing and murder, these people have got the idea of finding themselves a Messiah of their own; a Messiah who has and is all that which they themselves would like to have and be, but haven't and aren't. Up to that point I can understand the whole business perfectly well.

But on closer inspection it isn't quite so simple as that.

If their God really exists and let his only son be nailed to the cross at my instructions without giving me any indication, what sort of a god is that? I simply refuse to believe in a god capable of a trick like that.

This Jesus was a queer fellow, there's no doubt about that. He seemed rather helpless; he had a strange smile and he spoke confusedly (not a word of Greek!). But is that enough to allow a man to recognize him as the son of God? He wasn't very good-looking; rather ugly in fact, with a coarse, almost vulgar, face. He was pale and he looked ill; I didn't find him very interesting or attractive. If I hadn't happened to notice his hands I don't think I should have spoken to him at all. They were very long and very slim, and it wasn't easy to see what use they could possibly be to him. He couldn't have worked with them, for example—swung an axe, driven a saw, or carried a pitcher. And that's what the hands of such people are for. The executioner must have found it very easy to drive the nails through. Such hands won't have offered much resistance; that's quite certain. Perhaps there was very little blood in them. I shouldn't have been surprised at that.

I find it odd that I can remember him so clearly when I wasn't really much interested in him. Incidentally, their

God must be a fool to have produced such a wretched bundle of misery as his only begotten son!

That cat isn't getting any friendlier. She's missing for hours at a time, half the night sometimes, And she still eats only when she's alone. All the same, I like her because she is wild and independent. She doesn't make any concessions. Neither a good word nor a threatened cuff has any effect on her. She's got a mind of her own, and that's what I like about her. It would disappoint me if one day she got round to giving me her paw obediently.

My headaches are behaving differently. For one thing, they're becoming permanent. At one time it was enough to wait, to sleep a bit, or to lie down quietly for a while. Now they take no notice of that and dig themselves in firmly. Sometimes when I wake up in the morning I send Eleazar away and just lie there. How quickly people forget you! No one calls, none of my old colleagues, no officers, not even the friends of my wife. Just no one. I'm alone. I just don't exist any more. I'm simply not there. And if my name should ever crop up in a conversation (which it probably never does) then someone's bound to ask: "Pilate? You're not telling me *he's* still alive!"

Yes, I'm still alive.

XLVII

DEAR Claudia,

Forgive me, I need sympathy. I'm terribly alone, have a headache, and sit in my room and wait. I'd like to talk to a fellow human being, but there's no one to talk to. I'm scared of being hauled off for another interrogation. I call Eleazar, but he doesn't bother to come. What shall I do? Read, write, or go for a walk? When I read I get a headache. When I write I find myself thinking: 'What are you writing for?' When I go for a walk the people stare at me and whisper to each other: "Look, there's Pilate!" In my dream I call out to my mother, and she laughs at me. I don't believe in the Emperor or in the State, *or* in the mob. The world is obviously going to the dogs fast, so why do I bother to live on? It doesn't make sense. The sensation-mongers dominate politics, the swindlers make money, the whores make careers; women strip off their clothes and show themselves naked. Who speaks about whom, and how, isn't important; the important thing is that one *is* spoken about. At the circus the mob exults wildly, recklessly and frenziedly.

Hearts beg, brains freeze and souls are belaboured. Idiots cavort on the freak-market. What does it matter? We've got what it takes! When the neighbour has something, then the neighbour's neighbour must have more. The stupider the better! Whoever has slaves has credit too. Bribe someone to let you have a certificate to the effect that the Emperor loves you, and then buy yourself a house, a pet philosopher and a herd of cattle. In fact buy yourself anything you like. Say "my dear friend" to all, and think "You wretched nincompoop" of everyone.

"Family Life": Father has a fourteen-year old mistress; Mother carries on with the slave; the daughter has a married man and father of a family for a boy friend; and the son is a bit queer. The gods have withdrawn from the world, and have fun and games on their own. The

Senators spend their time in the circus, the whores pray, the priests make silly jokes, the Emperor behaves as though he were a god, the rich bathe in milk, slaves give the orders, poets remain silent, and the world is a very fine place. Vice parades in the parks and tramples on the flowers. Tears are sentimentality, thoughts are luxuries, money is mind, there is no recipe against headaches, and all's well with the world.

When a baby howls as soon as it sees the light of the world its mother says: "It's healthy!"

XLVIII

CHILDREN: adults without conformism.

XLIX

FOR the peace and freedom of Rome many crosses have been ordered.

Those who died on them died for nothing.

L

MAYBE I'm senile, but I'm not afraid of blood. Let it flow—but not into strong-boxes.

LI

WHAT these people want isn't altogether uninteresting, but they have no idea of religion.

I can't say I understood a great deal of it. A man, quite a sympathetic type if perhaps a trifle effeminate, read a sermon. The audience listened to him with absorption. I didn't much like their faces. It was in T.'s house. Incidentally I should never have dreamt of him as being a Christian! Most of those present were slaves. Things are going rapidly downhill with us. I stood there, a little at a loss perhaps. And as from the start I didn't feel very comfortable amongst them, I apologized several times for being there. Apparently they didn't mind one way or the other. They treated me just as they treated any other visitor, though perhaps on the whole they were a little more respectful to me. Though I'm sure that was more on account of my clothes than my standing. Their faces seemed to be asking: "What does he want amongst us?"

Eleazar did his best to smooth things over. He was very attentive to me, found me a good place, and seemed very pleased that I was there, and altogether blissfully happy. I had really hoped to hear something about Judea, about the Messianic idea and, above all, about the real aims of the Christians, but as far as I could make out the speaker was talking around these problems. He read a letter from a Pharisee named Paul, a chap who doesn't seem to have much sense. I've since heard that he tried his luck in Athens too, though with no more success.

The depressing thing about Christians is that they all sit around so dolefully. I watched them carefully. They hang on the lips of the speaker like young careerists eagerly trying to read the expression of the Emperor. They take everything the speaker says for granted, and they wouldn't dream of contradicting him. Of course, that's dangerous. Next to me sat a woman of the upper classes. I didn't know her. During the whole lecture she hardly stirred. She just sat there and stared at the speaker with her trembling lips a little parted. She seemed almost to be sucking the words out of his mouth. Her eyes were shining and she hardly dared to breathe. I found her behaviour a little disconcerting. People like that are fanatical, and fanatics are capable of anything.

There wasn't much to choose between the others. They were all motionless, all silent, all equally devout. All in all a very boring crowd.

The speaker got worked up and gesticulated a good deal. After a while I found myself asking what on earth I was doing in such company, but I consoled myself with the thought that it would be even more boring at home. I wasn't very happy, but at least I wasn't just sitting there and waiting for my headache to put in an appearance.

After the sermon, which was much too long, they all prayed. Then they crowded round the speaker, made a great fuss of him, and pumped his hand. Of course, no one dreamt of disagreeing with him. What he said pleased everyone.

Strange.

Many people wax just as enthusiastic at the rather

166

doubtful jokes you hear in the theatres nowadays. Well, which is the better?

What shall I do now?
I could look for the cat, of course, but she's pretty certain to be out.

LII

Dream:
I AM younger; perhaps fifty. I feel strong and vigorous. My hearing is excellent, and although I am sitting in my house in Rome I am not conscious of being retired. I am a gentleman and I have the appropriate power. I sit for a while at the table, and read or write. But then suddenly, for some reason or other, I get the idea that Claudia might have left me. It is night and I get up and search through all the rooms, calling out to her. But the whole house is empty. I am alone. I feel the sweat break out on my forehead. I grow giddy with panic, and I think to myself: 'You're dreaming.' But I'm not dreaming; Claudia isn't there any more. I look out to see whether it really is night. Of course, it's dark everywhere and the street is empty. I haven't made a mistake.

I run through the house shouting out, "Claudia! Claudia!" But there's no answer, and I run out into the street, still calling her name. After a while I find I've lost my way and don't know where I am. The sweat is running down my face, but I'm chilly all the same. And then an idea comes into my mind. I didn't look in Eleazar's room. She might be there! I rush back to the house. A man gets in my way. I stop and give him a second glance. He grins at me maliciously. I run on. After a while I look round to see whether the fellow is following me, and in doing so I trip and fall. I get up again, pass my hand over my forehead and find that it's bleeding. 'It doesn't matter,' I think, and I run on through the streets and alleyways until I finally get back to the house and go to Eleazar's room. It's empty.

I'm exhausted now, and I collapse. I rub the sweat, blood and fear from my forehead, but as soon as I have done so the pores seem to get larger and let double the amount of sweat, fear and blood through. I feel I can't go on. Everything is over. Suddenly I hear a noise, and I pull myself together and see that Eleazar has drawn my bath. I get undressed and get into the bath. The body breathes again, and suddenly I've forgotten everything. I don't even know any more that Claudia isn't there, and I feel bored. 'What will you do now?' I think. 'Perhaps dictate an urgent despatch to Burrus. It would be a good thing for him to get an urgent despatch. Otherwise he might get the idea that I'm doing nothing here in Caesarea but drinking wine and taking baths.'

I dried myself, forgot to dress, and went to Cassius, who no more noticed that I was naked than I did. "I've come to fetch my wife," I said. "She's not here," Cassius replied. 'That's odd,' I thought. And then I went to the Emperor. "Is my wife here?" I demanded. The Emperor looked at me and I noticed that he seemed scared. 'He's obviously got a bad conscience,' I thought. 'The fellow's betraying you with your wife. That's what it is!' I struck him in the face and he began to cry, threw himself down

168

and whimpered. And it was only then that I realized what I had done. I was scared at that and I stood there for a moment or two, petrified. 'The soldiers will rush in and seize you now,' I thought. I could almost feel the first blow on my head. It wasn't so bad as my headaches, though. I ran away, the soldiers after me. But I ran quicker than they did, and I managed to get home, where I intended to hide. I burst into Eleazar's room, and there I saw him kissing Claudia. I was speechless at the sight. Claudia smiled, stroked Eleazar's hair and said: "We are Christians." And she kissed him on both eyelids. I lost control of myself and was about to hurl myself at them when I woke up, with a terrible headache, with a pounding heart, and wet with sweat.

It took me three days to get over that dream. It's only now that I've got round to believing that Claudia didn't betray me, and that Eleazar isn't the lover type anyway. But for all that I still feel a little mistrustful.

LIII

AFTER exchanging observations in writing with Eleazar I've come to the conclusion that the thing that really shocks me most about the Christians is their misuse of the word "because". Their dialectical methods are extremely primitive. They make an assertion and then set out to prove it, but, by the time they've finished, the argument is more insecurely based than the original assertion. They also say that the authority of the Emperor is based on the will of God, and I take leave to doubt that very much.

Because, he says, God is his witness (a convenient witness, I must say!). *Because* He wants to save us (all right!). *Because* sin will be unable to exercise any power over us (why not?). *Because* he stakes himself, *because* he is quite certain, *because* of the mercy granted to him . . . (that's his business). *Because* God works through him. . . . And so on, and so on.

I don't much care for the whole business.

But two things do appeal to me as right enough:

1. "The good I desire I do not do; but the evil that I do not desire, I do."

That's how it always was with me where Claudia was concerned. I wanted to say: "You are the one I love," but what I said was: "You're cruel, or nasty, or mean."

2. "The kingdom of God is not eating and drinking, but righteousness and peace and joy in the Holy Spirit."

Good! But with that they won't get very far. The spirit is holy for perhaps two people in a hundred.

LIV

THE Christians have no "whys and wherefores". That's their weakness.

LV

But I'm not here to occupy myself with the Christians, though I must say they stimulate me.

I can't find any occupation for myself any more. What shall I do? 'You can get up and look into the sky,' I think.

I go back, sit down and write: "I looked up into the sky."

After a while I add: "The sky was blue."

If the sky had been grey or white, or dark or cloudy, I should have added: "The sky was grey—or white, or dark, or cloudy", as the case might be.

But what now?

'Claudia was a good wife,' I think.

All right, all right; I've realized that by this time. But the fact is she "was" a good wife, because now she's dead.

There's the cat, of course.

I get up.

She was lying near the heating asleep. But as I went to stroke her she leapt up, spat at me, and ran off.

So what?

What can I do now? Is there anything at all that interests me? What would give me pleasure at the moment? What am I writing for?

I am writing because for the time being I haven't a headache, because Claudia is dead, because the cat has run off, and because to do anything else would be even more boring than writing.

If this Jesus really was anything out of the ordinary then he didn't play fair with me. I asked him clear and definite questions, and he answered me in riddles. Was that fair?

And, in any case—the Jews just wanted a Messiah, and because they couldn't find a better one they took him. On the whole he suited them, because he was weak and yielding. His friends inflated his image and made a demigod out of him; and now they've got the nerve to carry his sayings as far as Rome. They're speculating on winning support from slaves and poor people, of course, because they say: "Before God all men are equal."

"All men equal?" If Socrates and Stephanio are equal before this god of theirs then they can keep him.

But what now?

Perhaps I could eat something. The trouble is that I don't feel in the least hungry.

If I think, perhaps something will occur to me that I shall take pleasure in writing down. Yesterday—or perhaps it would be the day before yesterday; I don't know any more—Eleazar told me about a man who murdered his wife. After he had handed her a goblet of poisoned wine he went off to visit a friend. There he sat down, chatted, drank wine, and made jokes. But after a while he said casually:

"By the way, my wife wasn't feeling very well when I went out. Perhaps I'd better go back now and see how she is."

"Oh, I shouldn't worry too much," said the friend lightly. "I expect she'll be all right. I don't suppose there's anything seriously wrong with her."

172

"I expect you're right," said the man, and he went on drinking and chatting, and flirting with a pretty dancer. A little later, however, he said to his friend:

"Would you do me a favour?"

"Why of course," replied the friend. "What is it?"

"Just send a slave over to my house to see that my wife's all right, will you, please?"

"Certainly," said the friend willingly, and he gave the necessary instructions to one of his slaves.

In the meantime the man went on amusing himself, and the dancer smiled promisingly at him.

Then the slave who had been sent out came back and reported that the wife of the man was lying there very still and quite stiff. It really looked as though she were dead, he said.

The man then burst into tears and refused to be comforted. He wept, and wept, saying: "She has done away with herself because I was unkind to her."

But three days later he confessed to the murder.

Is it worth while writing down a thing like that? Hardly.

I'd like to talk to someone though.

"How are you, Pilate?" I say to myself.

"Oh, I can't complain, you know," I reply.

"What about your headache these days?"

"Not too bad. They might be worse, I suppose."

"I'm sorry to hear there's been no improvement."

"Are you really?"

"Of course I am! What a question! Naturally I'm sorry about your headaches."

"I'm very glad if you're really sorry."

"And how's that cat of yours getting on? You know, the one . . ."

"Yes, of course. As a matter of fact I'm having a bit of bother with her. She's very timid, won't come near me. I don't think she likes me somehow."

"That's a shame, but if she's a nuisance why don't you just give her away? Or turn her out again?"

"Ah, no. Try to understand me: if I hadn't the cat any more—that is to say if I had nothing to get upset about—I shouldn't have anything left at all, you see."

"That's true, of course."

"I'm glad you understand."

"Yes, I certainly understand. By the way, I hear you went to a Christian meeting the other day. Whatever made you do that? Excuse me if I put it so bluntly, but you know that place inside out; you know the people there; and you're an expert where Messiahs are concerned. So how does it come about that you, of all people, take it into your head to go to a Christian meeting?"

"Oh, just one of those things. I happened to have nothing better to do at the time."

"I find that a bit difficult to believe."

"Do you? Well, they're quite nice people, you know. Or . . ."

"Or what?"

"Or do you think the Emperor's nice perhaps? Or actors? Or sensation-mongers? Or Senators?"

"No, no, of course not. You're right, certainly you're right."

"And then, I'm so much alone. I don't find it at all easy to put up with that."

"But that really depends on you, doesn't it? You must be a bit more cheerful. Close your eyes to a thing or two. Don't let it worry you so much. You know perfectly well the world's a wicked place, but you also know

174

you can't do anything about it, so why let it upset you? Go out more. Amuse yourself. You can't change the world."

"That's all very well for you," I reply. "You're different. I wouldn't mind being different either, but some rumour-monger or other stands at a street corner and whispers: 'Pilate's got Judea on his conscience.' And then the Emperor sends a secret agent into my house. The people who know me don't want to have anything to do with me any more; they know that I was recalled and that I'm in disfavour. And now I've actually been interrogated. Do you know what that means? If I say a word too much in the future then I'll be banished from the country, or even lose my head altogether. And as for the Christians, they say I crucified their Messiah. My wife is dead, and I treated her badly. Now my slave does just what he likes. No, the fact is I've got no desire to go on any more. And when on top of all that my headaches start . . ."

"You think too much, friend Pilate. And you take yourself too seriously."

"That'll do now. That's nonsense. You know perfectly well that I don't take myself too seriously. I won't have it."

"You can say what you like; that's your business. I'm only telling you . . ."

"You're only telling me: be more sensible, don't make a fuss, think on, go on, live on. I've heard it all before. But how? That's the point!"

"How should I know? I'm not you."

At that I gave the fellow up and went. You can't talk sensibly to a chap like that, so why try?

LVI

His name's Trajanus, and I found him a little too familiar. He had come on behalf of the Christian community, he said. I had, according to him, been placed in his care, and so he'd like to have a little chat with me. I pointed out that as I was practically deaf a chat with me wouldn't be very amusing for him; whereupon he replied that even the deaf could hear Christ's words. All right then.

Did I know Jesus, he wanted to know. It seemed to me that he was staging some sort of interrogation too, and I didn't much care for the idea. However . . .

"Oh, yes!" I replied, "as a matter of fact I knew him quite well. I actually sentenced him to death, you know."

"That was a great pity," he said.

"What was a great pity?" I asked.

"That you did that."

"My dear man," I objected. "Now you're really talking of things you don't know anything about. Were you ever in Judea?"

"No, I wasn't. But Jesus was the son of God."

"Have you seen his birth certificate?"

"No, of course not."

"Well?"

"Thus it is written."

"Where is it written?"

"Comrade Paul wrote it."

I told him that I wasn't much interested in what

Comrade Paul had written; and that, in any case, I knew already what he was going to say next—namely, that Jesus was the Messiah, that he had died for Barabbas and all other men, and that he had then risen from the dead, and was now sitting at the right hand of the Jewish God, in Heaven.

"That is so," he replied.

"We'll leave whether that's so or not without discussion," I said. "If you want to believe it, why not? But what's it got to do with me?"

"Don't you want to become a Christian?"

"How does one do that exactly?"

"By wanting the truth."

"Oh, I want the truth all right, but, with your permission, I find it a bit too much to accept that I should have committed a crime without knowing anything at all about it."

"You didn't recognize him for what he was?"

"I certainly did not recognize him for what you say he was."

"Then you were the only one."

'The only one,' I thought. 'The man's ignorance is quite appalling. These people manhandle the truth like a secret agent manhandling his victims,' but aloud I said: "Really? The only one, you think? But neither my officers nor my men, neither the priests nor the mob recognized this Jesus as the Messiah."

"The people suffered and wept and waited for the Messiah," he said.

"Maybe," I replied. "But the fact remains that it was the release of Barabbas they demanded."

"Then they didn't know what they were doing."

I became impatient. I have never had any time for

sophistries, and so I asked him point-blank what he wanted of me, whereupon he told me again that I had been entrusted to him.

"I don't mind that," I said, "but what's it got to do with me?"

If that's how things stood perhaps he'd better go now, he said. He could call on me again in a few days, and in the meantime I could think the matter over. Before leaving he assured me that every day not devoted to "the Lord" was a day wasted, and that he was really interested in my well-being.

Over-familiar, arrogant, and not at all to my liking.

LVII

PRAYER *at the grave of my wife* (written down and thus deprived of its value).

Blood flows through my veins, and I ask myself why. It knocks at the door of my heart, enters, makes its way through, and goes on again. Why? Runs into my feet, which are chilly; runs into my hands, which clench tight; runs into my brain and hammers there; remains there; and I think: 'You are staring at her grave now.' Yes, she's dead. Tears well up into my eyes. I close my eyes and I think. What about? I just don't know. The blood courses on. Frost seizes my backbone, shakes it thoroughly, and moves on. 'Oh, yes,' I think, 'she's dead.' I groan. The groan upsets me. I hear the wind, see weeds and a bird. Groan again. Yes, she *is* dead. The blood courses through my body; knocks at the door of my heart, enters, and courses on. It circulates. Now I stand there, see the winter breath condensing in the air, and ask myself: what are you really doing here? I don't know. It's too late. I could bend down and pull up weeds, but I can't see the point of that. I could pray perhaps, but instead I just stand around. What am I actually? Just something which stands around and thinks, and at intervals groans. I could think: 'I love her', but I don't. Thoughts began to whir. They buzz in my ears and I close my eyes. That's all. They buzz. Like wasps . . . And then they sting. I came to see the grave and think: 'Yes, yes, of course, it's Claudia's grave. Make yourself useful at least: pull out some of the weeds!' But no, it would be too banal to pull out weeds. I therefore remain silent and watch my breath condensing. I think and I sigh. Simply idiotic; idiotic the way things are. Come along, go home now. It's cold; there's no point in hanging around here. You might even catch cold. There's nothing you can do now, nothing you can change. But it's difficult just to go away like that. I look at the grave, read the inscription, and then say: "I'm going now, Claudia." But I still stand there. 'Stay just a bit longer,' I think. 'If you just walked away now she wouldn't understand it.' The soil is hard and glistening. Frost passes again and sends a shudder down my spine. 'Go home and look for your cat,' I think. 'Perhaps she's in the house now. Or you could read, or write. Now go! There's no sense in hanging around here, is there?'

So I take another look at the grave, read the inscription once more, notice the weeds again, take a deep breath in order to cut off the sigh before it rises, and think: 'Now don't be silly. Go home.' And in the end I do go, too scared to look round. What did I do at the grave then really? I just stood around.

LVIII

I WENT to the theatre. Not very extraordinary or original, I know, but I get too bored with doing the same things over and over again: feeding the cat, calling Eleazar, writing, visiting the grave, reading, and getting irritable. 'Claudia is dead,' I thought. 'All right. That's a fact to be reckoned with. Caesar was assassinated, Jesus was crucified, Socrates was made to drink the hemlock, and even Cassius is dead.' And I felt I had to get out, just get out; it didn't really matter where: into the street, into a brothel, into a drinking party, anywhere.

Very well, so I went to the theatre. I can't say I enjoyed it very much.

Of course, it isn't easy for the actors. There's so much competition nowadays. People prefer gladiatorial combats and circus games, animal baiting, mock sea-battles, and things of that sort; and it makes it very difficult for the theatre. The actors do their best to keep their end up. You'd think the best thing they could do would be to concentrate on the drama and the theatre proper, and avoid popular amusements as far as possible. But what does the theatre do nowadays? Exactly the opposite. It attempts to outdo the sensation-hunters, and it's not choosey about its methods either, descending even to the lowest obscenity.

I did my best to understand the piece I saw, but I didn't succeed, though I don't suppose that really mattered much. The title was "Country Life", and the characters were a cow, a boar, a goat, a messenger from the gods, and a young girl. I'm afraid I've forgotten the name of the author. And what happened in his play? The girl wants to find herself a husband. First she makes friends with the cow, but soon she notices that the cow's lesbian, and that doesn't suit her, so she moves on and falls in with a wild boar, which promptly rapes her. She doesn't much care for that either, so she presses on. She then meets a goat with which she falls madly in love, but the goat doesn't want to have anything to do with love, so again she's disappointed. But now at last the messenger from the gods appears to the young girl, explains just how complicated an affair love is, and offers her the chance of becoming the wife of a god. After so much disappointment the young girl is delighted at the idea. The nuptials take place. The girl now has a husband who is a god too. What more could she want? But in the night it turns out that the god is impotent. Too bad!

I don't know whether I've got it all quite right, but that was more or less the gist of the wretched thing.

After that there was a second piece. An actor played the death of Laureolus, who was crucified by the bodyguard of Caligula. By some trick or other an extraordinary amount of blood flowed from his hands when the nails were hammered through them, and this delighted the audience. In the meantime, whilst hanging from the cross, the man spat highly-seasoned smut into the pit. Round the cross were a number of naked actresses, and they sang and danced, and pretended to quarrel, pulling each other's hair out. And all amidst tremendous applause. You must see a thing like that to believe it.

Not so long ago the Emperor said that actors were an "invention of the evil spirits"; but that doesn't prevent him from sitting there and enjoying himself heartily. It obviously amuses him and he wants to see it too.

And the Christians try to tell me that the authority of the Emperor derives from the will of God! Fiddle-sticks! On the other hand you can almost be grateful to them for opposing the sort of things that go on in the theatre. Not that their disapproval does any good. When there's a big show on they might just as well shut up shop, because all their followers are sitting in the theatre with the others. Their lusts are just stronger than their belief in the Messiah.

I'd like to know what the dramatists really live on in Rome nowadays! Of course they give readings of their works, and we know that there is such a thing as a theatre dramatist. But can they really exist without the theatre?

LIX

Latrines:
I MUST correct myself. In answer to one of the questions put to me during my interrogation I suggested that it might be a good thing to open a few more latrines in Rome.

Since then I've changed my mind.

I was in town. I visited one or two temples and exhibitions of paintings, went to the cemeteries and all kinds of parks, and I can only say that the provision of latrines is excellently organized.

There are far more latrines available than there can possibly be any need for. This fact proves the cleanliness of our State and answers all those who talk of corruption.

Along the A. Wall I counted no fewer than 116 privies, of which seventeen were occupied; and even though I had the impression that they were not being used in accordance with their original intention, the will must take the place of the deed. And then our cloacal system functions excellently. The flushing both in private and public enclosures is beyond reproach. Despite all criticism, Rome breathes unobjectionable air, and whoever possesses a normal bladder can satisfy his needs anywhere and at any time.

The theatre privy was, as it happened, a little distance away, and under the earth. And there was a whore in front of the door. However, you don't have to use her. Of course, the State can't help that.[1]

LX

UNFORTUNATELY I've got round to the Christians again. What they want pleases me, I must say. They represent the only really interesting movement in our time. They live withdrawn from public life; they don't seek publicity; and although most of them come from very modest circumstances, they can be managed without calling in the military. Not that I'm altogether sure even now what it is they really believe in. Their God must be an angry God rather than a loving one, because when they think of him they are obviously more afraid than they are reassured. It is characteristic of their beliefs

[1] I can't help wondering if the former Governor is being ironical here. But I'm not sure.   L.P.B.

183

that they have taken over the Greek idea of immortality. Socrates, of course, says, and I quite agree with him, that death cannot be anything evil, but the Christians go further and say that life really starts only after death. An odd sort of belief, but, of course, you can understand it where slaves like Eleazar are concerned. "What have I had of life?" they ask themselves. And the answer is trouble, drubbings and boredom. They don't find it easy to believe that that's as it should be, so there's obviously something wrong. Aren't some slaves freed? Don't some people live in luxury? A slave wants a share in the good things too, so the only thing is for him to believe that he'll get it after death. It's simple enough.

But how on earth does anyone manage to believe in such a thing? It's a mystery to me. Barabbas I can understand at a pinch. He was to be crucified because he was a criminal. He denies that he was a criminal, of course, but the fact remains that according to Roman law he was. And now some other fellow comes along and dies instead of Barabbas. Naturally, Barabbas is deeply moved. He knows perfectly well that this Jesus is innocent, and he mingles with the crowd at the crucifixion, sees the dying glance of the crucified man, sees the watery blood oozing, sees the dry and cracked lips; and feels sorry for the chap hanging there on the cross and dying. And he thinks to himself: 'Actually I ought to be up there suffering, not him. God, what have I done!' And he turns to a man standing next to him and asks:

"Do you know the man?"

"Yes," says the other, "that's Jesus of Nazareth."

"What did he do? Why is he being crucified?"

"Don't you know?" demands the other. "He's dying for Barabbas, the rebel leader."

"Oh," says Barabbas. "I've heard of the man."

"And Jesus is the Messiah," says the other man.

"Do you really believe that?" queries Barabbas.

"Well, I didn't at first. But he prophesied his own death. He has also prophesied that he will rise again from the dead. And as he has already performed many miracles he'll probably perform that one too. And then we'll all have proof that he really is the Messiah."

All this makes Barabbas very confused. He looks at the dying Jesus, sees his head lolling forward on his chest, sees the trickling blood, the questioning eyes, the crown of thorns on his head. . . . And he stares with his mouth wide open in astonishment. His thoughts are wildly chaotic. He doesn't grasp it all yet; doesn't know what to believe. Swallows down a lump in his throat, and then turns again to the man beside him.

"He's dead now."

The other turns away. The show is over. But Barabbas stays on. He's already beginning to feel a bit frightened. Then he goes to the Temple and questions the Christians. On the third day he goes to the tomb and there he meets people talking eagerly about a miracle. . . . And gradually he finds himself beginning to believe.

All that's clear and logical. I'm not saying that Barabbas was right, but I can see and understand his point of view. But why should I believe it all just because the Emperor . . . .[1] You wouldn't call that a good reason, would you?

When we're a few more years further on and a certain

[1] I have been compelled to expunge these lines because of the serious *lèse-majesté* they contain. L.P.B.

185

amount of grass has grown over this legend that Jesus was the son of God, the Christians—if there still are any— will have got over their, so to speak, children's sicknesses, and by that time they will have clarified their beliefs.

LXI

Banditry:
ONE of my best men, an officer named L., disappeared one day whilst bearing a despatch into Jerusalem. He belonged to the unit stationed in Caesarea, and I would often send him into the city on such errands. There seemed little doubt that on the way he had fallen into the hands of bandits and been had carried off by them, or perhaps murdered and his body hidden. In any case he was missing.

Now Rome requires a report about every little thing that happens; but what sort of a report can you make when one of your officers just disappears from the face of the earth and neither you nor anyone else knows what's happened to him?

Of course, I could just have reported the truth, which would have looked something like this:

"For eight days now officer L. has been reported missing. He set off from Caesarea bearing an urgent despatch for Prefect Burrus in Jerusalem. But he never arrived there. I therefore officially report him as missing. The likelihood is that he fell a victim to bandits."

As I say, that would have been the plain, unvarnished

truth; but in Rome they're less interested in truth than in getting proper "reports", and anything as vague as that won't do. Rome wants clarity. So if I had sent in a report like that I should have received a reply in more or less the following terms:

"Confirm receipt of report referring to Officer L. Report does not state Officer L.'s present whereabouts. Please remedy omission. Further, you are hereby instructed to exterminate bandits systematically as from receipt of present. Please confirm."

In order to avoid such nonsensical exchanges I reported:

"Officer L. died of a fever, loyally serving Emperor and Rome. Will hold him always in honourable memory."

And to that Rome replied:

"All honour to Officer L. He will go into history as a hero."

And that was that. Incident closed. No more trouble. No one ever discovered what did actually happen to Officer L. And nobody inquired any further. He may have died of thirst, or been kicked to death, or despatched under some other form of torture. It's even possible that he was devoured by wild dogs. But you couldn't have reported anything like that. An officer who falls victim to ravenous dogs is unthinkable for Rome. Such a thing just does not and could not possibly happen. Therefore we allowed Officer L. to die of a fever in our loving care; and everyone was satisfied. And as for Officer L., if he had known he certainly wouldn't have minded, or have borne me any grudge on that account, because he was well acquainted with the bull. The false report suited the Emperor better than the truth would have done, the wife of Officer L. got her pension just the same and could still believe in the Roman Empire, and everyone proudly

mourned an officer lost in the course of duty—except
L. himself, and it isn't likely that we shall hear from him
again.

Sometimes it's very difficult to stay serious. I just
remember that I was going to write about banditry. It
existed in various forms:

(a) Ordinary robbers, i.e. common criminals
These were cowardly fellows, stupid too, and without
sufficient courage to plan deliberate murder. Their only
fear was to be found out and caught. They weren't
organized. They were just footpads carrying on their
ancient profession in the old-fashioned way. It hadn't
occurred to them to open fashionable marriage-broking
agencies.

(b) Tribal robbers
These were half-warriors, half-bandits, and quite
undisciplined. They just robbed everyone who fell into
their hands if he didn't belong to their own tribes. They
rarely killed their victims.

(c) Hired bands
These were mercenaries—paid and fed by the tribe;
they didn't need to work. Ready for action at a moment's
notice, their reward was their booty. They were ready to
fight for anyone, and their loyalty was invariably given
to the highest bidder. Cowardly. But there, what is done
for money always makes the doer cowardly.

(d) Fighter bands
Hostile to Rome. Bellus injustus. Politically indoc-
trinated, ruthless, and nationalistic to the core. Dangerous
because fanatical; not so much robbers as misled idealists.

A harmless Roman courier was more hateful to them than the Devil himself.

Rome ordered: "Exterminate banditry." Very well, so I reported: "Extermination almost completed. Judea becoming more and more friendly to Rome with every passing day."

LXII

VISIT from Trajanus. Christians seem to be persistent. The fellow has a round, rosy face, short, rather puffy hands, and a cheerful disposition. He wanted to read to me, but I wasn't willingly submitting to any such torture.

"I'm sorry," I said, "but I'm afraid I'm deaf. I wouldn't hear you."

Would I like to read for myself then? I had no objection to that so I told him to leave his literature behind and I would look through it at my leisure.

"You will get a great deal from it," he said.

"Possibly," I agreed, and I nodded.

"You can discover the True Belief and make the acquaintance of the True God in it."

"Oh, yes?"

It would inspire me, refresh my spirit and give me new hope, he went on.

That was wonderful, I said.

Of course, but God was bountiful.

Yes, yes, I agreed, he naturally would be. And in order to end the matter I thanked him for his trouble and asked him how the community was getting on.

Oh, the community was getting on very well, thank you. When was I coming to visit them again?

Well, I hadn't really thought about it. Should I?

I had heard the words of Paul last time, and listened to the voice of God. And Eleazar regarded me as an upright and honourable man. . . .

I told him that I was very much gratified to think that they attached so much importance to my slave's estimate of my character.

Hadn't the words of Paul made an impression on me? he wanted to know. Or did I still believe in the old heathen gods?

No, I certainly didn't.

In that case there was no further obstacle to my becoming a Christian. The community would be very glad to welcome me as a member.

That was very nice of them, but in fact I did not believe in their god either.

Why not?

I didn't see any reason why I should.

Because he was the one true God and he had revealed himself to man.

Which man?

All men.

I really couldn't say that he had revealed himself to me so far.

I was standing in my own light, he thought.

I then asked him if he would like a drink, but he refused. I had a drink myself, of course.

So he thought I was standing in my own light, did he? Well, that seemed quite reasonable; who else should if not myself?

There was always Jesus to be considered.

How much did he really know about this Jesus, I asked him. It would really be much better if he kept to the things and the people he really knew something about from personal experience. Frankly I was beginning to find all this talk about Jesus a little tiresome.

Why was I so irritable with him? he wanted to know.

Why? Because he would insist on talking of things he knew nothing whatever about.

"But Jesus is the son of God," he persisted.

"The son of God!" I repeated. They've got the nerve to say a thing like that to my face! "So that means that I had the son of God crucified, doesn't it?"

"Yes, but in the meantime God has forgiven you."

That just about took my breath away, and I told him to go. It was really a bit too much, and I didn't see why I should put up with it. I drank some more; cursed angrily; called Eleazar; looked for the cat, found her and sat down beside her on the floor.

"My dear cat," I began, "it appears that I crucified the son of God. Which means that if you've got a spark of decency left in that wiry body of yours you'll now get up and walk indignantly out of my house."

But she did nothing of the sort. She closed one eye completely, and she half-closed the other, and she purred. "Now you ought not to purr," I went on. "You ought to be afraid of me, and run away from me. Do you hear me?"

But she went on purring and looking at me through her half-closed eye.

'She's obviously not a Christian either,' I thought. I got up, drank some more wine and then went to sleep.

LXIII

Second talk with the cat:

"My dear cat: you came into my house because you were hungry. You were also mangy; and spiritually too you looked as though you'd had a bad time. I feed you, treat you fairly well, and your coat is no longer so shabby as it was at first. You just accept all this as a matter of course. You don't think of licking my hand because I feed you. Not you! And although I've never beaten you, you usually avoid me, and you spend whole nights out of the house. You obviously think: 'He feeds me. All right, so what?' And because that's the way you think and behave I like you.

"You know, sometimes I get headaches, sometimes I drink too much, and sometimes I think of my dead wife. In fact I think about a lot of things. Any ordinary day in my life now consists of a fistful of whys. You'd find that all very silly, and that's another reason why I like you. You catch a mouse, play with it for a while, then kill it and eat it. After that you lie down in the warmth and purr. As far as you're concerned that was a satisfactory day. Perhaps you had a friend and he left you. 'Very well,' you think: 'I'll just get myself another one.' Or you have kittens, and when they've caught their first mouse you tell them: 'Well, you're obviously quite old enough, go your own way from now on, find your own food and see how you get on. All the best!'

"Or you spot a fly buzzing around and you make a swipe at it, but the fly's too quick for you, so you say to yourself: 'I'm obviously not going to catch it; it's too quick for me. It's just teasing me. Let it buzz. I'll just stretch myself out, purr and go to sleep.' Or you notice that you've got to die; that everything is all over and there's nothing more for you. Or even if there is, there's nothing you can do about it, so why worry? So you go off and find yourself a quiet corner; and there you make yourself as comfortable as you can, lie on your side and stretch your legs out, breathe rather slower, give up the ghost and you're dead. Now I like that too.

"Dear cat, if only I could hold a conversation with you! You're dumb and I'm deaf, an almost ideal state of affairs. I should say to you: 'Now lazybones, how are you?'

"And you would answer: 'Leave me in peace. I want to sleep.'

" 'So, you want to sleep. But I want to talk to you.'

" 'Maybe you do, but what's that got to do with me? Please leave me in peace.'

" 'Don't be like that. I've always been good to you, haven't I? You've got to admit that.'

" 'I've not got to admit anything.'

" 'Do you deny it then?'

" 'For heaven's sake! Who said that I denied it? Do you always go on like this? All I've said so far is that I want to be left in peace and that for the moment I've no desire to let myself in for a conversation with you. If you don't understand a simple thing like that you can go to the Devil.'

" 'I suppose you haven't gone off your head a bit? The way you're talking to me! I never did!'

193

" 'Haven't you understood me? All I want is to be left in peace.'

" 'Now you listen to me . . .'

" 'What, that too!'

" 'Now that's rude. Just behave yourself, if you don't mind. I must say, at the moment your behaviour is abominable.'

" 'I've heard that sort of thing before. Just because you feel inclined to babble away to me I'm to go without my sleep. Who do you think I am?'

" 'A cat, as a matter of fact.'

" 'Would you believe it! You actually know that? Well, that's something at least, because you've been treating me as though I were an old boot, a convict, or your dead wife.'

" 'What's my wife got to do with it?'

" 'I just gave her as an example.'

" 'Well, don't. Keep her out of it.'

" 'As you please.' "

She looked at me with one eye for a moment or two, then closed it as though she were bored, and I could practically hear what she was thinking: 'Now for heaven's sake, clear off at last!'

"I think you're grossly impertinent," I said.

But she didn't react to that at all. So I tapped her on the nose until she consented to open one eye again.

"You're grossly impertinent. That's what I said. Didn't you hear me? What have you got to say to that? Am I deaf or are you? I said that you're grossly impertinent."

"Well, what about it?"

"You don't mind? You don't care?"

"Why should I care? Did you really think I cared? You're very naïve, I must say."

"That's the limit! Now if you don't . . ."

"All right! All right! Calm down, I'm getting up now. But if you aren't in too great a hurry to get rid of me let me stretch myself a bit first. You're a bit thick you know. You want to talk to me so you wake me up. You talk nonsense, without showing the slightest consideration for me—and when I say that just at the moment it doesn't suit me, you get nasty and threaten violence. The fact is you're a very disagreeable person."

"No, the fact is I've got no one else," I said. "But if you really want to sleep; all right. I'll leave you in peace."

"What's the use of that now? I'm already awake anyway. So you can save your breath."

With that she got up, stretched herself, arched her back, probably thought me a silly old fogey, and then stalked off leaving me on my own.

Of course, I could lock her in; but then it really would be all over between us.

LXIV

THERE was a fire in one of the western districts of the town last night. Eleazar says over seventy houses were burnt down. But as no particular friend of the Emperor's, and no popular gladiator, lost his life in the fire, nothing official is being said about it. A few houses will be rebuilt "more beautiful than before", and that's the end of that. Victims. About four hundred dead, they say. But there are so many people in Rome they won't be missed.

I went down to the Tiber, sat down on a stone and looked at the water, and . . . And what? Nothing really. I just thought. What I thought about? Claudia, of course. Anything else? I think the sight of moving water encourages thoughts. My thoughts go to Claudia, to the sea, to a face I knew during my term of office in Judea—it was the face of Burrus. And then for a while nothing at all. Then Claudia again; her tear-stained face; an outburst of anger; the night she died . . . But I don't want to think of that. Then my thoughts go to Eleazar, to Cassius, to Stephanio, to a drunken soldier in the park at Caesarea—why does one recall such unimportant things as that so clearly? And then to my father, at a time when he happened to be scolding me; to a lad I saw at the house of Cassius, a small dark-haired little fellow who didn't understand the obscenities they had taught him to sing. And then to a night ride from Jerusalem to Caesarea; I was scared in case bandits should attack us, but above all I was very anxious not to show that I was scared. Then I looked consciously at the moving water again, felt cold, shivered, and got up.

Soon after we met for the first time Claudia and I went down to the Tiber together. It was in high summer and we found ourselves a place on the bank where we were alone. The bank was stony; there were a lot of reeds and clouds of midges.

"I like it here," I said.

I didn't really like it at all there. The current was much too strong for bathing, and there were far too many reeds and other tangled growth around. The real advantage was that we were alone. There was no one around to spy on us, hear what we said to each other, see what we did.

"It's rather stony here," she said.

So I took the stones one after the other and threw them into the water until I had cleared a place for us to lie down. We lay there for a while side by side, and then I took her hand. We looked up into the sky and we heard the noise of the river as it swept on towards the sea. The sun was powerful.

"It's very hot," said Claudia after a while.

"Yes, it is, isn't it," I said. I was in love with her. She got up.

"What are you going to do?" I asked.

"I'm too hot. I'm going to take my clothes off."

"Good," I said, "So will I."

And we went back into the bushes and undressed. I was finished long before she was, I thought, and I waited.

"Where are you?" I called out after a while.

But then I saw her. She was already lying down by the river again, naked, with her hands behind her head and her eyes closed. I looked at her. 'She's very beautiful,' I thought.

"What are you doing so long?" she called out.

"Nothing," I said, and I went behind her. "I'll look for a few stones."

"Isn't it lovely here?" she said.

"Lovely," I agreed.

I looked around for stones, but I was thinking of Claudia all the time. I walked along the river bank, picked up stones and threw them into the water and watched the ripples they made. I knew that I mustn't go too close to Claudia at the moment. She was too beautiful.

"What are you doing?" she called out.

I made no reply.

She sat up, and her breasts were more rounded than ever like that.

"Why are you so far away?" she asked.

"Oh, nothing."

She stood up and came over to where I had sat down and she bent over me and I saw her breasts close by and smelt her hair.

"What's the matter with you?" she asked.

"Nothing. Nothing," I replied. "Shall we go now?"

She didn't understand me.

"If you like," she said.

On the way back we were silent. Then finally she asked: "Don't you like me any more?"

"Yes, of course I do."

"Well, then . . ."

What does "well, then" mean now?

She's dead.

LXV

I'M gradually getting thoroughly sick and tired of it. Barabbas comes, Trajanus comes, some officer or the other comes, the charwoman comes . . . And they're all interested in the same thing:

"Now, Pilate, you were in Jerusalem at the time. You ought to know all about it. They're saying this Jesus was the son of God: what's the truth of the matter?"

All right! All right! So I've taken the trouble to look

out my old notes, correspondence files, reports and official records again, and although I can't reconstruct the case again exactly at this distance of time—after all, you'd be buried in paper if you tried to keep a detailed file of everyone you have to deal with—I'll do my best.

Interrogation of Jesus:

First of all, there was nothing particularly striking or significant about the man. He might have been anybody. He was innocent, of course. In that respect I have no intention of defending myself. All I have to say about that is this:

1. If I had acquitted him the local politicians would have denounced me in Rome again. I already held proofs that they intended to petition the Emperor against me on the ground that I had *once again* ignored an imperial decree. The interesting thing about this plan was that they intended to accuse me of *lèse-majesté*.

2. The Emperor didn't know his business. He issued orders which were impossible to carry out. When he added: "It will be done in this way", that usually meant in reality that it couldn't possibly be done in that way.

3. I didn't want to try Jesus at all; it was the local politicians who wanted that. And still less did I want to convict the man.

4. The Nazarene himself made things very difficult for me. He wasn't very adroit or polished. If you asked him: "Would you care for a drink of water?", he would reply bluntly: "I'm not thirsty." And when I asked him if there was anything I could do for him, he merely said that no one could do anything for him.

The fact is that if a man is determined to die, as he was, there's nothing you can do about it.

5. My instructions on the point were quite definite. I had to send a report on the matter to Rome, and this I did. And Rome made no objections whatever.

6. The process was not exclusively political; there was a religious background. The High Priests, and in particular their leaders, Annas and Caiaphas, obviously found this "Messiah" a nuisance. Apparently he wasn't sufficiently respectful to them so they wanted to get rid of him.

For this reason I sought from the start to edge the case from the political into the religious sphere. Religious affairs—so far as they did not impinge on my political, juridical and administrative duties—were no concern of mine. I didn't care what the Jews believed in: a God, a dog, an ape with eight tails . . . As far as I was concerned they could believe in anything they liked provided it did not endanger the interests of the State.

7. I did not succeed. Those who accused him were obstinate. When I asked, "What has he done? Is he a criminal?" they answered: "Yes, he is a criminal; he is stirring up the people to refuse to pay taxes."

"I have no evidence on that point," I replied, "but as you are charging him, presumably you have, so tell me what crime he is to be charged with?"

They assured me that they were honourable men, and that if Jesus were not a criminal they would not dream of accusing him.

But that naturally wasn't good enough for me. I knew Caiaphas and his friends.

"If he has done something which does not suit you," I declared, "then take him away and try him according to your own laws. It is no concern of mine."

8. At first they agreed to this proposal, but only, as it turned out later, to adjust their subsequent tactics.

When they returned they declared that he was a criminal guilty of a capital crime. They knew that I was not in a position to refuse to try a man accused on a capital charge. However, I knew from my Chiliarch that Jesus was not guilty either of planning insurrection or of calling on the people to refuse to pay taxes. He was quite harmless. Therefore I asked him if he were the Messiah.

In return he wanted to know whether I knew that on my own or whether others had told me. Of course, it isn't in order to answer the questions of a Governor with a counter-question. All the same I replied: "The Sanhedrim have condemned you, and now they have brought you before a Roman court. I am giving you an opportunity to defend yourself, and therefore I ask you whether you are the Messiah."

He then said that he was the Messiah, and that he had come into the world to proclaim the truth. Everyone who wanted the truth would listen to his voice.

I was very pleased with this reply, because such things were nothing to do with me. Truth? What is truth? I then went outside to his accusers and told them that Jesus was not a rebel and that his aims were exclusively of a religious nature, and thus no concern of mine. They were therefore to take him away.

9. But they remained obstinate and refused to give way, though their arguments became more and more threadbare as they went along. But I did not allow myself to be side-tracked. During the course of the negotiations something was said which just suited my book. One of the accusers called out that Jesus came from Galilee, and, as everyone knew, all the rebels came from Galilee. I seized on that observation at once and declared that in that case I was not competent to deal with the matter;

it was obviously a case for Herod. They should therefore take the man to him to be dealt with, since the affair was no concern of mine.

To bother your head about such trivialities is, of course, a sign of senility.

LXVI

THERE was a drunk on the street. His friends had been drinking too, but they were not as far gone as he was. He was getting quarrelsome.

I looked on.

They seized him, restrained him, and tried to persuade him to calm down, but he still wanted to fight. An old woman came up and talked to him as you might to a small child, stroking him on the cheek. In reply he struck her in the face.

Someone shouted: "But you can't strike your old mother!"

"What?" he bellowed. "I can't, can't I! I can, and a good deal more besides." And he did his best to break loose from the grip of his friends. He shouted, cursed, struggled and kicked, but they held on.

The old woman turned away, leant against the wall of a house and wept.

'Very sad,' I thought, and I took my goblet and poured myself out some more wine.

I haven't a mother any more. If I had one I would think: 'Drink up! She's still there.'

But now I've no one at all, and so I think? 'Drink up!
They're all dead!'

It's much the same.

LXVII

Interrogation of Jesus (continued):

10. Herod refused to try Jesus. Particularly because he
was highly amused to see that they were so furious with
the man. They therefore dragged him back to me.

It's so often depressing that no one is prepared to take
the responsibility. One pushes it on to the other. Very
well, obviously this man Jesus was a bit of a nuisance, but
was that a good reason for crucifying him? The Pharisees
found him dangerous because he had become too powerful. They feared his rivalry. They felt that when he spoke
of his God he believed what he said, whereas all they
believed in was position, power and money.

The so-called Freedom Fighters didn't much care for
him either. At first they had thought to turn him into a
figurehead, but it was not long before they were compelled to recognize that he had no talent at all for that
sort of thing. They wanted him to say that his divine
mission was directed against Rome and Roman domina-
tion, but he refused to say that; he had a will of his own.
That made them furious so that they too were in favour
of getting rid of him. But none of them was willing to
take the responsibility for his death. They were all too
cowardly for that.

I wonder if my cat has picked up something some-where. Poison perhaps? She's asleep, but she's writhing a bit and she seems to be in pain.

LXVIII

I'VE had a headache now for thirty-six hours on end. I've been lying down, sleeping, worrying things over, imagining all sorts of things. Against the possibility of suicide for me is the consideration that then someone will come and clear away my things; the last word. No, I don't care for the idea of that.

LXIX

I WENT to the Christians again. Trajanus welcomed me like a brother, told me he was delighted to see me, and that one couldn't do too much in honour of God.

The proceedings were the same as usual. They sat around rather dolefully and listened to the sermon. Of course, I didn't understand a thing. But I felt myself being watched. They looked over at me when they thought I wasn't looking. They talked about me; and when one, who thought himself unobserved, pointed at me, his interlocutor went as white as a sheet. I wonder what goes on inside the heads of these people. Do they *really* think I murdered their god? They must be a little queer in the head. And if they really do think that why do they take such pains with me instead of turning me out? Are they too cowardly, or too clever? Why the devil did I let Eleazar persuade me to come again? 'Damn the man!' I thought.

There were slaves next to me. Times change. They all knew me very well, but didn't show it. They were a bit shy of coming too close to me and I noticed them staring at my hands. Did they expect to see the blood of their Jesus on them? Now and again they looked at my face, but when I caught their glances they looked away at once and pretended to be absorbed in the sermon. They could dissemble very cleverly, and that annoyed me. I closed my eyes: darkness, deafness. I thought of Claudia. She made me promise to acquit Jesus, and I convicted him nevertheless. She had a very disagreeable dream, it appeared, and Jesus played a role in it. Anyway, she cried all day and kept begging me not to convict him. In the end I promised.

It was always the same; if I left her in Caesarea alone she was anxious and scared, she didn't sleep and she would cry a good deal. And when I returned I had all I could do to soothe her down. But if I took her with me she felt uncomfortable too, and wanted to get back to Caesarea. Or she'd feel a great desire for the sea, and a nostalgia for Rome. She always wanted to have everything to hand, and nothing must ever change for her. If a slave broke a favourite vase she'd mourn over it for days, and hardly look at the slave who had done it. Her longing was like that too; it was for a vase, an ornament, a tree. In particular she always felt uncomfortable within

205

the walls of the Antonia. She could never get enough air, she said.

When she heard that I had condemned Jesus after all, she wept, accused me of breaking my word to her, and demanded that we should go back to Caesarea at once. But it was no better when we got there. I pointed out very reasonably that I had had no choice in the matter. I had done all I possibly could to avoid condemning the man. And then she asked who *was* the ruler of this wretched country then? I tried to explain the situation to her. Of course I was the Governor of Judea and therefore in that sense the ruler, but for all that the Jews were still a power to be reckoned with in their own country. If I had acquitted the man they would have sent their Roman advocate to the Emperor, and that might have had very disagreeable consequences for us. It was quite on the cards then that the Emperor would recall me, even banish me perhaps. In any case it would mean that she and I would have to part. Did she want that? No, of course not, she replied. But the Emperor would have to be just. What would things come to if the Emperor himself were no longer just?

The Emperor just! He wasn't just and he never had been. But how explain that to her?

I opened my eyes, and a slave who had been quite close to me started back. I take it he had been staring into my face and thinking to himself: 'Look, Pilate is asleep.' But I hadn't been asleep. I had merely been thinking with my eyes closed. Sleeping isn't as simple as some people think.

I began to feel more and more uncomfortable. I could sense from the atmosphere around me that they suspected me not merely of passing a verdict which was forced on me (which wouldn't have been so bad) but of a horrible crime. I felt like breaking out and striking left and right; shouting at them, hitting them in their silent mouths, and letting them have it straight from the shoulder:

"I know you don't like me, so don't pretend you do! But now I'm going to have my say and tell you a thing or two. Hundreds of thousands of Jews come into Jerusalem at the Feast of the Passover. Do you understand what that means? It was my duty as Roman Governor to uphold law and order. Just that and nothing more. And the Jews had a privilege, a privilege the Emperor himself had granted them. At the Feast of the Passover they were entitled to demand the release of a prisoner, and I as Governor had no power to refuse. I had to release the man they named. I wanted them to take Jesus, but they wouldn't. I used all my powers of persuasion to get them to ask for him, but it was no good; they wouldn't have him. They wanted someone else, a fellow named Barabbas. I know you're going to say that I oughtn't to have done it all the same, because Jesus was innocent. I know he was innocent; and I knew then that he was innocent. There was never any question about it. But do you know what would have happened if I had acted against the will of the people? They would have rioted. There would have been stone-throwing. The Freedom Party would have risen in revolt. The Sanhedrim would have stirred up the mob. There would have been street-fighting. And then not merely one innocent person would have died, but a hundred, perhaps five hundred, a thousand—impossible to say how many. And, because I had only very few of them, my soldiers would have had to act ruthlessly to suppress the disorders. Then Rome would have wanted to know how the whole thing blew up in the first place, how such a thing could possibly happen. And what should I have been compelled to answer? *'It all happened because I did not carry out the orders of the Emperor.'*

"But you just won't understand that. You don't want to. You just 'believe'. And therefore talking to you is like talking to a brick wall."

He wanted to die, of that there's no doubt whatever. And seeing that he wanted to die was I under any obligation to wrap him up in cotton-wool and defend him against Caiaphas and his friends? What do they imagine the job of a Governor in an occupied country is like?

After the sermon I left the place. I had had enough. I could stand neither the atmosphere nor the faces around me. Trajanus came running after me and caught me up in the street, asking me rather anxiously why I had hurried off so quickly. Why? "Just because you don't like me; any of you."

That answer made him sad and me angry.

LXX

Interrogation of Jesus (continued):
A FEW years before I became Governor of Judea, the Legate of Syria, Quintilius Varus, crushed an insurrection there, and on one single day he caused two thousand rebels to be crucified. Later on he committed suicide somewhere in the North. But that's neither here

nor there: such measures are sometimes necessary.

The course of the further proceedings:

More and more people had gathered. There were pilgrims, sightseers, organized bawlers, and in general a very mixed rabble. However, I was glad that I hadn't to negotiate with the Sanhedrim on their own. I thought to myself: 'The whole of Jerusalem cheered this Jesus, and believed in him and his divine mission. After all, he had performed miracles, or so they said.' So I asked whether they wanted me to release their Messiah king.

No, they didn't. That rattled me. It was a mystery, and it still is to this day for me. How was it possible that they wanted to see their own fellow-countryman crucified when I was quite prepared to release him? What went on in their minds? Did they just *want* to see blood? Did they suddenly hate this man?

At first I really assumed that they hadn't understood me properly. I had been so confident that I had just asked them straight out, without any long preliminaries, whether they wanted me to release Jesus. I now repeated my question. And they all shouted, "No! No! Crucify him!"

To-day, of course, I realize that to some extent the people who shouted were put up to it by Barabbas and by the Sanhedrim. And there was another thing I ought to have thought of—namely, that they would naturally have been prejudiced against any suggestion of mine, because they hated Rome and everything connected with it.

However, I didn't give way, and because I regarded it as the only hope now, I ordered the scourging.

LXXI

MET Stephanio on the street.

He greeted me, smiled in an embarrassed sort of way, and went on.

I can't remember what I did.

LXXII

Interrogation of Jesus (continued):
I DID not have him scourged before the eyes of the people, but in the vestibule of the Praetorium. I had not as yet finally condemned him and I was still determined not to give way to the demands of the mob and of those Sanhedrim rogues. 'When the people see the flayed and bleeding wretch,' I thought, 'they'll take pity on him. Their lust for blood will be satisfied, and they won't want me to crucify him.' In this way I hoped to get round the necessity for a conviction.

But even then they refused to budge. I repeated that I regarded him as innocent; told them once again that they should take him away and do what they liked with him. He was nothing to do with me. But I had no success. They shouted, waved their arms, and shook their fists at me. More and more people came up and the mob got wilder and wilder. They were demanding to know whether the Emperor had given them a law or not, and whether I intended to trample on it. They shouted that they hadn't a Messiah king and that they were loyal to the Roman Emperor, and whether I was. That, of course, was quite disconcerting.

I took Jesus away back into the building, leaving the mob to cool its heels outside. They growled dangerously behind me and it obviously wasn't going to be easy. And then, as I have said, he was determined to die; which made the whole thing senseless. However, after a while I went outside and declared that I was breaking off the proceedings and proposed to release the prisoner. At that they openly threatened that they would charge me before the Emperor with *lèse-majesté*; and they weren't very respectful about it either.

And they would have done too! I thought of Claudia and of my promise to her. And I thought of my career, and even of my life itself. For a moment or two I felt giddy. 'He's innocent,' I thought. 'I know that, but many other people who've died have been innocent too.' I looked at the faces before me; they were pale, grim and sinister. And I felt alone, absolutely alone. It was no use holding out any longer. . . .

"Take him," I said.

LXXIII

Two or three nights ago I had some sort of an attack. I don't myself really know what it was. But I'm calmer now. Eleazar is urging me to call in a doctor, but I'm afraid to. Who could I trust now anyway? I know Verrus very well from former days, but I don't know how he stands with me now. If he happens to be in favour with the Emperor then my life won't be of much value to him. And if he attached too little importance to my life then in his hands I might very easily die a little earlier than I would otherwise have done, and despite everything I don't much care for that prospect.

I take it that I recovered consciousness when it was all over. I found myself lying on the floor and having difficulty with my breathing. I was sweating and shivering at the same time. I thought I was dying, of course, but the odd thing was that it didn't disturb me very much. My heart was beating so hard that I could feel the hammering in my ears. I wanted to shout, but my tongue refused its service. I put my hands to my heart and then to my forehead, and they were suddenly damp and hot. I put them palm down on the ground to cool them, and then I tried to push myself into a sitting position that way, but I hadn't enough strength. I tried to shout again, but I couldn't get a sound out. 'It's really all up with me,' I thought, and it was then that I began to get scared; an uncomfortable feeling of fear moved my belly.

I opened my eyes wide and stared at the smooth, ice-cold ceiling, and my eyes seemed to flicker, and there were many tiny dancing stars. 'No,' I thought, 'I don't want to die!' Again I tried to push myself up, again without success. 'All right then,' I thought; 'then the other thing'; and I relaxed and all the remaining strength seemed to ooze out of my body into the floor, holding me fast as though by suction. 'Very well,' I thought, 'just die then. At least you'll have peace at last, a wonderful, uninterrupted peace.' When I opened my eyes again Eleazar was bending over me anxiously and thinking of fetching a doctor. "No, not that," I said.

And now I'm afraid to go to sleep at all. But the trouble is that going to sleep was my only real specific against those headaches.

So I've tried drinking more instead, but the drinking only brings the headaches on more quickly.

I suppose the best thing to do is nothing at all?

But my thoughts . . .

LXXIV

A NEW year has begun.

Everyone's wishing the other a good New Year.

By "good" they mean prosperous, healthy and happy. And they do the same thing every year, year after year until they die.

Then they wonder: when did we actually live?

LXXV

Self-analysis:
THE findings are largely negative where I'm concerned.
I can't summon up much interest in myself, which is a
pity really because I'd very much like to find myself
interesting. When I was young I often persuaded myself
that I was born for something out of the ordinary. It
wasn't true of course. The culmination of my career was
my appointment as Governor of a small and not very
important province. Such talents as I possessed remained
hardly used. During my life I spent most of my time in
civil service departments during the day and salons in the
evening, holding a pen in the one case and a goblet of
wine in the other, and keeping my thoughts to myself.
Heaven knows what's happened to all those thoughts
now; they're suspended somewhere up in the air, a col-
lection of partly-good and partly-silly ideas. But that's
all over anyway.

My failings are almost indescribable and almost innumerable. But on the spur of the moment I can think
of quite a number. I'm brutal, weak, timid, lazy, dog-
matic, vague, obstinate, without ambition, without
goodness of heart, without any real joy in living, indulgent
to my own faults, ruthless to charlatans, squeamish, for-
getful, ungrateful, unjust, extravagant, reckless; and as
far as I'm concerned, just insufferable.

On the other hand, I'm also loyal and truthful; though

to be perfectly frank, rather than go hungry, be thirsty, see myself banished, or allow myself to be stoned, I'd willingly abandon all loyalty and all truthfulness. I'm afraid of dying. It isn't the state of being dead that worries me. I wouldn't mind that at all. Then my eyes would be blind, my lips would be dumb, and my ears would really be deaf. All that wouldn't bother me in the least. But to breathe, and in breathing have to think: 'You're not going to manage the next breath.' Or you might have strength enough to draw in your next breath, but not strength enough to expel it again. 'No, you're not going to manage that.' Now that's what I'm frightened of. And when I get scared, and feel it there just above the heart, my breath comes more quickly and louder as I deliberately try to get past that dividing line between "in" and "out", "in" and "out", "in" and "out". But there's bound to come a moment when I won't manage the trick any more; and that's what I'm afraid of.

My brain is in order; at least, I think it is. I know that some people think differently, but that doesn't matter. My brain regards a thought in my cups as more import-ant than a speech by the Emperor. And that isn't because I regard myself as particularly clever—"perish the thought", as the Christians would say in their jargon—but simply because the Emperor is such a stupid man.

My brain gives me plenty to do all the time, and I'm grateful to it for that. My legs are often tired, my eyes often ache, my heart is often heavy, but my brain at least is always busy. It thinks, keeps me occupied, gets headaches, and thinks over what I need: more wine, a new pen. Or may be it thinks about an argument or about a dream. And it's always right. My hands want to stroke the cat, but the cat slips out of them. My heart turns to Claudia, but she is dead. That is to say, my hands and my heart make mistakes, but not my brain.

It possesses three milliard slaves. Thoughts they're called. It sends the one to Rome, the other to Caesarea, the third to the sea, the fourth to the tub of Diogenes, the fifth to the wife of Cassius. . . . The 317th it sends to heaven; the 680th to my cat, the 1,350th to Jesus of Nazareth; and some other thought to someone else. And my thoughts aren't accommodating. They know no mercy and no forgiveness. They come unbidden, look at me, and go again. They aren't concerned with what I do with them. They don't bother in the least about that.

They're stubborn too. As soon as I start "doing" something they get lazy and bored. They don't like that, so the best thing to do is nothing, and let them come.

Now my heart, as far as I can judge, is relatively normal. When my thoughts excite me it seems to get a little uncertain, but I don't take its behaviour very seriously then. My heart is naturally inclined to exaggerate. It sees blood and closes my eyes and makes me think: 'Is this blood necessary?' Then thought number 710 answers: 'Of course it's necessary! This blood must flow.' After which my heart calms down and thinks: 'Well, it wasn't your blood anyway.'

In some situations my heart finds the rest of me too brutal, and I don't care to interfere; but I must say I think my heart could be a bit more considerate. If it came to the point my thoughts would take the whole world under their wing; not so my heart. It has a will of its own, sticks its toes in, and decides: 'No, I won't give way; not in a thousand years!' Not even when all my thoughts from number one to number 30,000 all try to

216

persuade it. Which means that my heart is more heartless than any of my thoughts.

But my thoughts won't be expressed. As soon as I open my mouth to get rid of them my tongue forms them according to its own taste. For this reason I don't care much for my tongue; it's too loose, and it's balanced too precariously between my brain and heart.

I don't like my heart much. I don't much care for my eyes either. They retain far too much nonsense. They record the puffy features of the Emperor and the wobbling head of the drunken Cassius. They have no feeling for essentials. For example, they can't remember what colour my cat's eyes are.

Now my ears are all right. They're deaf.

I have the usual number of internal organs, of course; but the only ones I have any direct knowledge of are my stomach, my bladder and my right kidney. I got to know my stomach because it's been upset on innumerable occasions, either by eating or drinking too much; my bladder because it occasionally catches cold; and my right kidney because there's something wrong with it so that from time to time it gives me a stabbing pain. I don't know the other organs because I've never felt them.

But with my head it's different; I feel it almost all the time; it hurts and it propounds many riddles.

Myself, for example?

I grasp many things too late. I'm not satisfied with myself. Sometimes I lie about myself; but that's because the things I know about myself don't please me and I'd sooner not have them true.

I have good taste and a good memory, in which I live very willingly.

In these times you can't really live anywhere else

anyway; you can only go on breathing, try to find yourself a place somewhere on the periphery and have nothing
to do with it all.

LXXVI

THE day before yesterday on a walk down to the Tiber I
met the wife of Verrus. I didn't know whether she wanted
to have anything to do with me so I nodded to her and
was walking on when she stopped me and started to talk.
We were standing on the street and she talked into my
ear, but I still didn't understand her. Then she asked me to
come into the house. I don't know whether she did that
because she realized that I was deaf, or because she didn't
want to be seen talking to me on the street. Anyway, I
went into the house with her. My first thought was
whether I ought to let her husband examine me after all.

I don't really know what his reputation as a doctor is
to-day, but when we were both young everyone prophesied a great future for him.

It is a fact that I do hear better in enclosed premises.
Outside it's probably the many other noises in the street,
the footsteps, the talk of the passers-by, and so on that
confuse my hearing. It may also be that I find it more
difficult to concentrate outdoors than in.

The wife of Verrus had hardly changed, I found. 'And
Claudia's dead,' I thought.

"Claudia has been dead some time now," she said
after a while.

I nodded.

"She was a fine person."

"Yes, of course."

"You keep her grave well tended, Pilate. I must say that for you."

"Yes, I do."

"You know, she was here three days before she died. And how very much alive she was! Who would have thought that her end would come so quickly? We were laughing and chatting together so light-heartedly."

"Were you?"

"Yes. No, she really was a fine person."

"Yes, she certainly was."

Slight pause.

"But what about you?" she went on. "What are you doing with yourself now?"

"Oh, thank you, I'm keeping well."

"Yes, I must say, you're looking well."

"Really?"

"Yes, so fresh and so calm."

"As a matter of fact I was thinking of consulting your husband."

"Oh, what's the matter with you then? Are you in pain?"

"Not at the moment, but I *will* come to see him I think."

"Yes, do that. And apart from your health?"

"Well, you know my position. People don't fall over themselves to know me."

"But, Pilate! What nonsense you're talking! You're very welcome here any time you care to come, you know that. Do you think that just because the Emperor recalled you from Judea that makes any difference to our friendship? Whatever can you think of us! No, on the contrary: you're always a very welcome guest in our house."

"Thank you," I said. "Thank you very much."

"By the way, if you want to see my husband professionally come in the evening, please. He has so much to do during the day; and, in any case, it isn't necessary that everyone should know that you're his patient."

"No, of course not," I said, and made to go.

"Ah, poor Claudia," she said. "Sometimes she was so annoyed with you."

"I know that," I admitted.

"She couldn't have harmed a fly though."

"No, she couldn't have done."

"All those years she had to spend abroad didn't do her health any good, you know; that's quite certain. Don't you think it would have been better to send her back to Rome every few months?"

"Perhaps it would have been."

"Who knows whether in that case . . ."

"Quite, but I liked to have her with me."

"Yes, I suppose you're like all the men, terribly selfish."

"I don't know that it was selfishness really; you see, I loved her."

"I didn't think you two had got on as well as all that."

"Didn't you?"

"But, Pilate, you know as well as I do how often she was here and in tears about you!"

"Really?" I said, and this time I got up to go.

"And when you visit my husband; don't forget, come in the evening."

"Yes, of course," I said. "In order that people needn't know I'm your husband's patient."

"And don't forget: you're welcome here whenever you care to come."

"No, I won't forget. Thank you very much."

LXXVII

"I'm worried about my cat."

"Worried?"

"Yes, worried. She's losing her hair rather too freely, it seems to me."

"And you're worried about that?"

"Naturally."

"Naturally? But why?"

"Well, I don't really know why. Do you think I ought to feel worried about the sickness of the Emperor instead?"

"Yes, that would be more sensible."

"Why?"

LXXVIII

Talk with my cat:

"What are you thinking about, cat?"

"Nothing."

"How do you manage that?"

"Oh, I just purr, twitch my ears and close my eyes."

"And beyond that?"

"What do you mean: 'beyond that'? Beyond that I don't do anything at all."

"But you must have something or other in your mind."

"No, I mustn't. Why?"

"Well, one's always thinking of something or other."

"I don't know anything about that. I think only when I have to. When I see a mouse I think to myself at once: you want that mouse, get it! But sometimes I notice that the mouse is too cunning for me, and then I don't bother."

"You don't even try to think out how it is the mouse is too cunning for you?"

"No. What good would that do?"

"I'd find that too slothful."

"Hark, who's talking! You're too lazy to go and fetch yourself a goblet when you want to drink."

"All the same, I do think."

"What do you think about then?"

"About my wife."

"But she's dead."

"About the Emperor then."

"What good is that?"

"Or about life in general."

"Anything else?"

"Yes, I think about myself, about my faults, my weaknesses and my troubles."

"Anything else?"

"Now look here, stop that silly 'Anything else'."

"All right, all right. You can think about anything you like, of course; that's your affair, but don't start picking a quarrel with me again."

"I'm not picking a quarrel. But I must admit that your indifference does provoke me."

"I'm not in the least indifferent. On the contrary. Do you think I haven't my own troubles? It's just that I don't make such a fuss about them as you do about yours."

"I'd like your troubles! Ridiculous!"

"If you don't mind we won't talk about my troubles. You haven't the faintest idea about them and I'll look after them on my own."

"I'm very curious to know what they are, all the same. You could tell me."

"Of course I could, but why should I?"

"Well, because there's a bond between us. We belong together, you and I. You're all I have now."

"There's probably some very good reason why no one else likes you. Perhaps you're too inconsiderate?"

"If I were so very inconsiderate would I look after you as I do?"

"Look after me? What do you mean: look after me?"

"Well, I feed you, don't I?"

"That's nice of you, but if you want to keep a cat you have to give it food, don't you?"

"I could just as well let you go hungry."

"Do you think you could? The fact is, I wouldn't go hungry whatever you did. I'd just go off and find myself other quarters. And you'd be completely alone then."

"The fact is, I'm fond of you."

"Yes, but only because you don't want to be alone. There's no real affection there. That's all nonsense."

"Oho, so you understand something about affection, do you?"

"Of course I do. I just don't talk about it much; that's all."

"Tell me about just one of your troubles though."

"No. Certainly not. I am as I am, and that's how I shall always be."

"I'd give you something nice if you did, something really special."

"I'm not to be bribed."

"If you tell me I'll promise never to talk to you again. You'll have your peace and quiet once and for all, and then you can do exactly as you like. Is that a deal?"

"Very well then: I had a miscarriage once."

"I'm sorry to hear about that."

"It was only about three weeks ago."

"Was it painful?"

"I don't care to talk about it any more."

"Very well."

"And no more talk of any kind. You promised that, remember."

"And I'll keep my word."

LXXIX

Discussion with Trajanus:

"JESUS was taken in the Garden of Olives, wasn't he?" Trajanus asked.

"Could be," I replied.

"Well, that's how it was reported afterwards: He was there deep in prayer with three of his disciples when a traitor brought along the soldiers to arrest him."

"It could have been like that."

"How is it you seem so uncertain about it all? You were the Governor at the time weren't you?"

"Yes, of course, but I didn't interfere in the internal affairs of the country except to maintain law and order."

"Who was in charge of the soldiers then?"

"How should I know? They were probably men of the Sanhedrim acting under the orders of Annas or Caiaphas. Probably Caiaphas, because Jesus was brought before him in the first place."

"They weren't Roman soldiers then?"

"No, they weren't."

At that he said that he wasn't quite sure that he thoroughly understood the situation. Would I be prepared to answer a few questions?

It depended on the questions, I said.

"Well, for example, who had any interest in the arrest of Jesus apart from the Romans?"

"The Romans had no interest in the arrest of Jesus; but the Pharisees, the Scribes, the High Priests, the Saducees, and the Sanhedrim had. And perhaps the followers of Herod."

"What had they against him?"

"He was growing too popular for their liking, and therefore dangerous."

"But was that bad?"

"Of course it was, from their point of view."

"Anything else?"

"Well, they accused him of associating with whores and publicans."

"Why shouldn't he have done? After all, he was the Messiah."

"I didn't mind, but the orthodox pietists thought differently about it."

"How then?"

"He was in their way. And they wanted money."

"Money?"

"Yes, money."

"Although they were pious?"

"Well, they regarded themselves as pious, and the people took their word for it."

"What money was that?"

"Well, you see, they sold sacrificial requisites, and their piety gave them credit. Incidentally, the business was very well organized. They praised God and at the same time their bellies got larger. They were so pious that even their hanging jowls swung to and fro in God's praise."

"Do you mean that seriously?"

"No, not really; just ironically."

"But Jesus was different, wasn't he?"

"Yes, indeed he was. For example, he had no belly—at least, not in that sense."

"What did he look like?"

"Thin, angular and rather unattractive."

"Apart from that, were there any divine signs—compelling eyes, or a mysterious voice?"

"Nothing at all that I noticed."

"But he performed miracles, didn't he?"

"His enemies said he was in league with the Devil."

"But he faced his enemies openly?"

"No, as a matter of fact he didn't. He was in Jerusalem secretly on a number of occasions, and he was never prepared to give a straight answer to a straight question; he always evaded the issue. I knew about it every time he was in Jerusalem, but as far as I was concerned he was doing no harm, and I therefore took no action against him."

"So the Romans didn't arrest him, even though that's what is said?"

"Lots of things are said, but that doesn't make them true. If I had ordered his arrest he would have been taken to a Roman prison."

"Are you sure about that?"

"Sure about it! Let me tell you that no man I ever had arrested could possibly have been handed over to a creature like Caiaphas. What do you take me for?"

At that he apologized and declared that he hadn't meant anything offensive.

I was pleased to hear it, I said irritably. But it was a bit too much to suggest that I would have a man arrested and then play him into the hands of rogues and villains.

Once again he assured me that he hadn't meant it like that at all.

"Well, how did you mean it then?"

"In all friendship and neighbourly Christian love."

"I see."

LXXX

Discussion with Trajanus (continued):
"DID you ever speak privately with Jesus?"

"Yes, I did. Incidentally, I've got a headache. My headaches are steadily getting worse, and more and more difficult to put up with."

Who was my doctor? he wanted to know.

I told him I hadn't one; I didn't trust them.

But there were quite a number of good doctors in Rome. For example, I should go to . . . He mentioned a name. He was certainly a good man. Incidentally, his wife was a Christian.

"What's his wife got to do with it?" I demanded.

"Oh, nothing! But he's a good doctor."

"Because his wife's a Christian?"

"No, of course not."

"Why did you mention it then?"

"Oh, no particular reason. Just so."

"I see."

At that he said I really was distrustful, too distrustful. But if I agreed we would now talk about the Messiah, the son of God.

Did he mean Jesus? I wanted to know.

"Yes." Had I spoken with him in private with no one else present, for example?

"Yes, I did. I asked him where he came from, and whether he had ordinary human parents or was of divine origin. But I can't remember any more what he replied."

"The very fact that you asked him such questions is significant. He must have made a deep impression on you, because you certainly don't ask any ordinary person whether he is of divine origin, do you?"

"No, naturally you don't ask any ordinary person questions like that, but I did so in this case only because it was necessary for my juridical argument."

"How, exactly?"

"Well, if I could show that his aims were of a religious nature then I had shown at the same time that the whole affair was no concern of mine."

"Didn't you feel anything strange or out of the ordinary at the time?"

"Why should I have done?" I countered.

And I went on to say that it was only he, Trajanus, and

his friends who were now gradually making the man a trifle uncanny for me.

That at least was some progress, he thought.

Progress in what direction? I wanted to know.

Towards the true faith.

"I see."

"Did you talk to him about other things as well?"

"Yes, of course I did. I can't remember the details any more, but he was certainly full of his divine mission."

"Some people here in Rome say that you threatened him."

"What should I have threatened him with and why?"

"With death on the cross, because you certainly had that power, hadn't you?"

"Yes, of course I had, but go on."

"If God had so willed he could have deprived you of that power though."

"Well, as he didn't, he obviously didn't want to?"

"That is so."

"And if I visited the community again, what then?"

"Everyone would be very glad to see you."

"Frankly, I can't say that that's my impression; rather the contrary: I felt that my presence was disagreeable to them; and, after all, that's understandable enough."

"No one bears you any ill-will. I can assure you of that."

"Outwardly perhaps you're right, but inwardly, in their hearts—that's a different matter."

"I'm afraid you're not willing to let anyone help you."

"Oh, you're quite wrong there. But how is anyone to help me?"

LXXXI

THERE's no question about it, hundreds of thousands cheered him. At last they had their Messiah. But I miscalculated. I wanted to make the proceedings short. He was innocent, and I had nothing to hold against him. I therefore asked them immediately: "Do you want me to release Jesus?"

I was fully confident, you see. Of course, they could have chosen another man from amongst those awaiting death, that was their perfect right. I knew that. But I didn't doubt for one moment that they would choose Jesus. And therefore I asked myself what was the point of beating about the bush: the sooner the matter was settled, the better for everyone concerned.

But I was wrong; they didn't want him. Now why on earth was that? One might well ask! Of course, the priests had great power, and when they condemned him the people must have become confused and uncertain. They were more inclined to believe the priests than God himself. Were the people so afraid of the powerful ones who sat in the Temple then? Were their own convictions of less importance to them than a condescending glance from the priestly centre of power? In any case, I had certainly miscalculated.

I know that I am guilty, but that's my affair. It's something I've got to settle with myself and no one else in the world. But beyond that I also know that there was only one person concerned who did not want the death of Jesus; and that one person was Pilate.

Now, Claudia, you begged me not to give way, you must remember that. You said: "Don't do this man any harm." Do you remember?

I promised, and you told me that you had had a terrible dream. You urged me to listen to you and be kind to the man.

But I love you, Claudia. The wife of Verrus said the other day that she thought we hadn't got on all that well together, but that doesn't make any difference to the fact that I loved you. And I knew perfectly well in this particular case that I was personally involved and would have to pay the piper myself. It is true that I could have acquitted him as you wanted me to, and I did do my best. It is also true that I did not treat him brutally; you can be quite sure of that. But in the major decision I had no alternative. There are sometimes moments when even the chief himself must give way. One isn't *the* chief either as Governor or as God himself. A man is never his own chief.

Even now, so long after, I believe that I recognized the danger at once. The Emperor was not in a very good mood in those days. Only a few weeks before he had caused his best friend to be executed. And what for? Just because the man was of a different opinion from that held by his Imperial friend. That's all.

To have acquitted the man Jesus against the will of the people, the local authorities, the High Priests, and even of the accused himself, an acquittal which would have been against both the interests of Rome and the law of the Emperor! What do you think that would have cost me?

Very likely my head, though perhaps just banishment. And what would that have meant? I would have lost you, Claudia; lost you sooner and in even more terrible circumstances.

Very well, I didn't want that. I should have been prepared to risk banishment, I think. I'm not saying that I should have been prepared to risk my head, mark you; despite the intolerable pain it gives me from time to time. I'm too fond of it. And in any case I have no desire to play the hero, and I never have had.

LXXXII

HEADACHE. Persistent, unflagging. Hours, days, nights. How much longer?

They're trampling. Why? It doesn't matter to you why. When it pleases them they trample. And it does please them to trample. That's all.

LXXXIII

ELEAZAR wanted to know whether I had tortured his Jesus for very long.

"What do you mean exactly?"

"Well, you had him scourged, and there were no witnesses."

"There also aren't any witnesses to the fact that you don't bother much about me any more."

"I am always there to do your bidding, master," he said.

"Is that so? Well, last night I shouted myself hoarse after you and you didn't come."

"I didn't hear you calling."

"Small wonder! You weren't there; you were with your fellow Christians."

"We were praying together."

"And in the meantime I had another attack."

"I'm very sorry about that, master."

"That's touching of you."

"Did you have him severely scourged?"

"So you're not interested in the fact that when I need you you're not there. A fine servant you are! Any master would fall over himself to have a servant like you!"

"There is only one master."

"And what does *he* pay you with?"

"He pays with peace and happiness."

"And does that fill your belly?"

"Yes. When I think on him everything is good."

"Very well, then think on him for a few days and see if it satisfies your belly."

"I would gladly starve for him."

"Well, why don't you then?"

"I want to help you, master."

"You want to help me!"

"Yes, master. You see, you are good."

"I see. By the way, where's my cat?"

"Yesterday I saw her in your room."

"Yesterday! But where is she to-day?"

"I don't know, master. But she'll return."

"Because I'm good, I suppose?"

"Yes, master."

"What makes you think I'm good—if you really do?"

"You were never bad to me."

"That's no argument. You should ask the Emperor, ask Cassius, ask your Jesus, ask Trajanus, ask my dead wife. They'll all tell you a very different story."

"Did you have him severely scourged?"

"No, I didn't."

"But they say that he looked terrible when it was over."

"Of course he did. But he stood the crucifixion afterwards for half an hour, and he wasn't a strong man. Do you think he would have managed that if I had had him scourged really severely?"

"No, I suppose not. But what is the truth then?"

"There you go again! Truth! Quite simply, the truth is far removed from what is generally believed."

LXXXIV

Dream:
I MUST die. My breath pumps my lungs full of air and supports the heart, but the heart stands still. 'Now's the time,' I thought. 'I'm going to die.' And I waited.

Nothing happened. My lungs were full of air, my heart stood still, and my eyes stared fixedly at a spot on the wall. 'Something's just got to happen soon,' I thought. But it didn't.

Disagreeable to lie there so foolishly and just wait. I tried to open my mouth and call for Eleazar, but once again it refused service. Naturally, a mouth doesn't function when a man's dead. It's one of those things you have to get used to. I continued staring at the wall, listening. My head was quite clear.

"Breathe," it said to my lungs.

But my lungs were disinclined to obey.

"Start beating again," it said to my heart.

But my heart refused to co-operate.

Then my body tried to turn over to one side, but it didn't succeed. I sweated and felt very sticky.

'Well, this does seem to be the end of it,' I thought.

'But perhaps Claudia will come?'

That thought encouraged me. I wouldn't mind being dead if Claudia were to come and stroke my forehead. I lay there and wondered what she looked like now. Had she perhaps changed much since I had last seen her?

But she didn't come. No one came, and I just lay there and waited.

Then quite suddenly they were in the room. At first I didn't recognize them. They seized me roughly and flung me to the ground. I wanted to shout, but I couldn't shout any more. They didn't handle me very gently. They just banged me on my back with a thud, and I heard one of them say: "He's a stiff; he won't feel anything any more."

I couldn't move.

Then another one said: "Where's the nails?"

This one dragged my arms up and knelt on my chest so that I couldn't breathe any more. I wanted to protest:

"What are you doing to me? How dare you?"

"Here are the nails," said another one.

235

The man who was kneeling on my chest dragged open the fingers of one hand and drove a nail through the palm. I noticed that his breath stank.

"What do you think you're doing to me?" I managed to gasp, but the man didn't seem to hear. He hammered the nail through the palm of my hand savagely. I noticed that the sweat was standing out in beads on his forehead.

'I wonder what he's so angry about,' I thought.

He hammered away at the nail. It was already firmly fixed, I could feel that. But he still went on hammering.

'That's odd,' I thought. 'I wonder why he's doing that?'

Then he took the other hand and tore the fingers open in the same way, took another nail, put it into position and then hammered it home. He seemed to be growing more angry than ever.

'All right, let him get on with it if he must,' I thought, 'but what's it all about?' The worst part of it all was his stinking breath.

'When he's finished with your hand he'll drive nails through your feet,' I thought. 'And then you'll be hanging; hanging on the floor.'

But after that, what?

I lay on the floor and stared at a spot on the ceiling, and the man who had been kneeling on my chest now bent low over me and shouted into my ear: "Are you a Christian now?"

"Yes," I replied, "I'm a Christian now."

"What!" he exclaimed. "You're still not a Christian? I'll soon show you." And he kicked me in the face.

"But I said 'yes'," I replied. "What do you want of me?"

"I'll teach you to say 'no' when you ought to say 'yes',"

he shouted, and thereupon he kicked me in the face again.

"Don't you understand," I asked. "I did say 'yes'; I did say that I was a Christian now."

Obviously he didn't understand me, for he kicked me in the face a third time.

My cat now came up and began licking the nails. She didn't lick my hands, just the nails.

"Hallo!" I said. "Is that you?"

But she went away.

I lay there crucified on the floor, and the man who had driven the nails in so angrily and had then kicked me several times in the face bent over me again, and suddenly I saw that it was Trajanus. Then the second man came closer.

'Would you believe it?' I thought. 'It's Eleazar!'

And then the third one came up.

"Claudia!" I exclaimed. "You too?"

"Why not?" she asked.

At that I went off to sleep again.

LXXXV

I ought to go and see an oculist.

LXXXVI

My cat came and sprang on to my lap, and that pleased me very much. I stroked her.

"You're a nice cat," I said.

"Well, I've gradually got used to you," she replied.

"You've no idea how much that pleases me," I said.

"It pleases me too," she said, looked at me for a moment, then closed her eyes and began to purr.

"Do you want to go to sleep?" I asked.

But she made no reply, just sat there with closed eyes and purred. I didn't dare to move, and I sat there like that for an hour, or half the day—I don't know any more how long it actually was. I could feel her purring in my hands. Then quite suddenly she opened her eyes, blinked at me, stretched first one leg and then the other, and finally all four at once, opened her mouth and yawned, shook herself awake and then sprang down to the ground.

"Well, did you have a nice sleep?" I asked.

She arched her back and stalked off.

LXXXVII

Supposing he really did have a god for his father, what about it? Why didn't he give me a sign? And by the way, how did Burrus come to make an official report about those strange happenings in the Temple and in the skies? Did Jesus really rise again from the dead? And how did he manage to make sick people well again? But if his father really was a god, how could this god bear to see his son bleeding to death on the cross? And how does it come about that his blood takes away my sins? And another thing: Why did he choose to appear in that out-of-the-way province, and not in Rome? Where is he now? Oughtn't his followers to have died with him? Why did they abandon him? And why did he allow himself to be humiliated? If he had to die why did he choose that particular fashion: through vainglorious priests, my unwilling sentence, and at the hands of common soldiers? And why has he so many followers now? Why do they believe in him? And why do I now remember so many details in connection with him in particular? And, above all, how does it come about that here I am at this distance seriously considering the whole fantastic business? Am I growing senile? Haven't we our own Emperor? But the Emperor is a liar.

Now if Jesus really was the son of God why didn't he make everyone who came into contact with him feel it? Why is it that you *can* believe in him but you don't *have* to? How is it that there are other gods side by side with him? Why does he allow men to worship money, power and luxury instead of him? When he said that a new life begins after death for all of us, why didn't he give us some idea of what it would be like? And why were his words always so puzzling? How is it possible that he let himself be betrayed? Is his god bloodthirsty then? If Jesus is alive and dwelling somewhere why doesn't he work some kind of miracle for us all to see, such as striking all thieves blind? Why isn't he logical? When he says: "Love your enemies as yourself", how does it come about that I hate myself? If he has great power, why does he hide it? And why, if he has died for them and brought them salvation, are all his followers so doleful? Don't they understand him perhaps? Why, for example, didn't he say to me: "I am the son of God, and therefore not of this world, and therefore I advise you not to sacrifice me to the mob?" The answer to that question at least is quite clear: he had to die. But why did he pick out me for the purpose? Was that fair? Did he want to test my conscience perhaps? How was I to know what he was? What were his motives? What has he done, and what offence have I committed?

LXXXVIII

FOR weeks now I have been unable to do anything more than lie on my back.

The only one who visits me still is Trajanus.

I haven't had any more attacks though.

LXXXIX

I'M a little better. I can't remember any more how it was. When I opened my eyes Verrus was bending over me. I recognized him again at once.

"What's the matter with me?" I demanded.

He shook his head, pushed me gently back on to the bed and put his finger to his lips. I looked at him. I couldn't remember a thing. Then I saw Eleazar. 'They're not thinking of poisoning you, I suppose,' I thought.

At that I sat up and shouted at them: "What have you done to me?"

At that they seized me and forced me back onto the bed. I tried to resist, but, of course, they were stronger than I was, so they succeeded. 'They really have poisoned you,' I thought.

And I've been lying there like that for weeks now. Sometimes Trajanus comes and sits with me. Verrus says that I have caught an infection in the head, and that such things take some time to cure. But what can you believe nowadays?

I sleep most of the time, and then I have extraordinary dreams.

There are spots and stains on the ceiling, and cracks and even holes in it. If I look at them for a long time they become shapes: hands, cats, long necks, and so on. Every day there are different outlines.

This morning I even saw Claudia's head.

But I can't find the place any more.

Verrus says that I shouldn't try to write again until I'm quite well. For the time being I should just rest.

"How many weeks have I been lying here like this?" I asked Eleazar.

"You'll be better soon, master," he replied.

Replied? What sort of a reply is that?

I'm wondering whether it would be a good idea to

give my jottings to Trajanus. Eleazar tells me that Claudia's grave is being kept neat and tidy. I wonder if that's true? And, in any case, it isn't enough just to pull the weeds out.

To-day I saw a hand on the ceiling. The fingers were gnarled, and between the bones the flesh was like paper. Like a bird's claw. I closed my eyes, and then opened them again: closed, opened, closed, opened. And then I saw the hand move.

My headaches are no longer so bad. I really am getting very much better.

I don't understand why Verrus still forbids me to get up. What's the idea behind it? And why does he look so strangely at me? Yesterday he asked me how my wife was.

"My wife?" I said. "Why she's dead."

"Really?" he replied. "She's really dead?"

Now that was a silly question. He knows perfectly well she's dead.

Verrus said he'd like to see my notes. I must be very careful.

"How's Claudia?" I asked Eleazar.

"Her grave is kept in the best order," he replied.

"What's in the best order?"

"Her grave, master."

"I didn't ask you about her grave, I asked you about her, how she was."

"Don't excite yourself unnecessarily, master."

And with that he took me by the shoulders and pushed me back on to the bed, as though I were his slave and not he mine. And I'm too weak to defend myself. All the same, my headaches are getting better with every passing day. And there will come a time when I shall be able to revenge myself on them all.

Where is my cat?

Verrus says the cat's ill and his wife is looking after it. Eleazar says she's around somewhere and I shouldn't bother my head about her. And Trajanus said: "Your cat? Oh yes, your cat. She's on the street I think. Yes, that's right, I saw her just now on the street."

Obviously, there's something wrong.

Got up. It was easier than I thought. Afterwards I said to Verrus:

"I think I'm strong enough to get up a bit now."

"Oh, no," he replied, "out of the question."

But it's not out of the question at all. But why is he so anxious that I shouldn't get up? Why does he positively forbid me even to attempt it? What's he up to with me? Oh, I think I can imagine; I wasn't exactly born yesterday.

I must be even more careful than before.

"Look," I said to Verrus, "there are figures on the ceiling."

"So there are," he agreed.

But I wasn't satisfied with that. "Can you really see them?" I demanded. "What can you see up there?"

He hesitated. I noticed that particularly.

"Well," he said, "I can see a face."

"What sort of a face?"

"It's the face of your wife."

But it wasn't; it was an eye. The left eye of my cat.

Now why does Verrus lie to me? He wants to poison

243

me; I've known that for a long time. But why does he keep on postponing it?

I must find out the reason.

If Verrus wants to poison me then he'll go about it very carefully. He isn't a fool, so it isn't likely that he'll poison me himself. And he may have an idea that I am very watchful and on my guard.

He'll therefore find someone to do it for him. Now who would that be.

Eleazar, of course. And that means that from now on I mustn't accept anything to drink from him.

"You mustn't get up, master."

"Why not, Eleazar?"

"Because you've only just had another attack."

"When was that?"

"The night before last, master."

"Now that's not true, I know. The night before last I dreamt about my death. I can remember that very clearly."

Eleazar made no further reply. He is one of those who are planning to get rid of me.

Trajanus was here. On account of my deafness it isn't easy for us to chat, although I'm hearing better every day now. He said the community was prospering and that everyone wished me well.

He poured me out wine, although Verrus has forbidden me to have any. Trajanus probably realizes that Verrus forbids everything that might do me any good.

Verrus is a dangerous man. If Trajanus really wishes me well, why doesn't he find me another doctor?

Eleazar brought me a goblet with something to drink.

"You drink from it first," I said.

He stammered something and tried to lie his way out of it, saying that it was my medicine, and that I was ill, not he.

I struck him in the face.

He mustn't think that I shall let him poison me quite as easily as that.

Jesus was a good man. But the others, the many others?

I can't find out what's happened to my cat. Perhaps they tried the poison on her that they afterwards intend for me?

"Are you angry with me, Eleazar, because I struck you?"

"You didn't strike me, master."

"What! Have you forgotten already? I struck you in the face because you tried to poison me. It was yesterday. No, perhaps it was the day before. Don't you remember?"

"Be calm, master."

How is it that he can't remember it any more. I shouldn't have thought that possible. Or perhaps he's only pretending not to remember. *He* ought to go to a doctor, but not to Verrus.

Every day I hide my notes somewhere else, because I know that when I'm asleep they look for them. They don't find them though, because I'm cleverer than all of them put together.

Claudia came to me yesterday and said: "There, you see! I'm here again."

She hasn't changed.

I could have asked her where she had been all this long time, but, of course, I know that she's been dead.

As I didn't want to offend her, I said simply: "I'm glad you're there again, Claudia."

She looked at me. I could see that she still loved me. I wanted to get up, take her by the hand, and say how delighted I was, but just at that moment Eleazar came into the room.

"What do you want?" I demanded.

"Master, you mustn't get up," he said.

"Can't you see that I'm talking to my wife. How dare you interrupt us?"

"Master, you mustn't get up," he repeated.

"I wish to talk to my wife. Can't you see that? And, in any case, greet her properly."

He took no notice, and that made me very angry.

"Master," he said.

"Stop that damned 'Master' here and 'Master' there. Greet my wife properly as I tell you. Or are you blind perhaps?"

He just looked at me, but he didn't do as I said. I don't know what's come over him. I must certainly think about the matter carefully. He is becoming very impertinent, shameless and even violent. I caught hold of him, dragged him over to Claudia, threw him to the ground and shouted: "Will you greet my wife now?"

He still didn't obey me.

"Let him be," said Claudia. "He doesn't mean it like that."

"I insist that he greets you properly. I refuse to tolerate such behaviour."

"Come," said Claudia. "Lie down again."

She drew me away, helped me to get back into bed, and then kissed me on the forehead.

She is good to me.

Eleazar was still kneeling on the floor.

"Go away," I said irritably. "I don't want to see you again . . . ever."

At that he rose and went. But I know that he's up to something, something dangerous.

When we were alone Claudia took my hand, looked at me, kissed me, and said that my headaches would not come back any more.

'She hasn't changed in the least,' I thought.

"You are a good Christian," she said.

"Me?" I said in astonishment. "No, I'm not a Christian. Where did you get that idea from?"

"You must just have faith."

"Faith in what, Claudia?"

"In the Resurrection, for example."

"I'm to believe that he rose from the dead after I sentenced him and had him crucified?"

"Yes. Is it so difficult then?"

"It's very difficult indeed."

"You love me, don't you," she said, "and you believe what I say. Well, why won't you believe with me then?"

"Because it's just impossible."

She remained silent and stroked my forehead.

"You are good to me," I said.

She made no reply, but went on looking at me.

"Oh!" she exclaimed, and she kissed my forehead, my lips, my neck and my eyelids; "it would be wonderful if you became a Christian. Oh, that would be lovely!" And she kissed my forehead, my hands and my ears, and kept on talking. But I didn't understand her. She talked about God and Jesus, and love and charity. But I still didn't understand her. "Write it all down," I said. "I've become so deaf; I can't understand properly any more."

But she talked on, stroking my face. "But I can't under-you," I said in a louder voice. "I'm deaf. Write it down for me." But she didn't write it down; she didn't seem to hear me; she just went on talking. I could see her lips moving rapidly, and I watched them. I could understand "God", and "Jesus", and "the Holy Spirit". And when she said "the Holy Spirit" it looked very funny, and I laughed. "Write it down," I said again loudly, but she still didn't hear me and went on talking. In the end the blood rushed to my head and I became angry, raised myself up and shouted at her.

Eleazar and Verrus must have heard me shouting because now they rushed into the room, seized me and forced me back on to the bed and held me there, whilst I shouted: "Claudia! Claudia! Help me!" But she made no attempt to help me. She had no compassion for me. I then said that I wanted to speak to Trajanus. They should go and get Trajanus at once, because I had told him that I wanted to become a Christian.

"What are you trying to do with me?" I shouted. "I want to become a Christian."

But they still held me. They almost throttled me, in fact. But Trajanus did come. I don't know where from. I asked him to help me, but he wouldn't either. None of them would help me. They've killed my cat between them and now they want to kill me too, and I can't defend myself.

"Let me go!" I shouted. "Let me go!"

But they didn't let me go. Then Verrus said: "It's over now," and I demanded what it was that was over, but he didn't answer and went out of the room. Eleazar followed him, leaving Trajanus behind with me.

"What's the position now?" I demanded. "What does

the community say? Am I to become a Christian? Will you have me?"

But he was evasive. He tried to calm me down, and to avoid an answer that way, but I insisted and I shouted: "I demand an answer. Tell me the truth. What is the truth?" I caught hold of him and clung to him, shook him; even tried to kill him, but I was much too weak for that. "What is truth?" I demanded, but all he would say was: "You must first get well again, and then we'll talk about it. But calm down now." But I didn't want to calm down, I wanted the truth there and then. "The truth is that you don't want me," I shouted angrily. "You want to poison me. Admit it! Why don't you admit it?" And I shook him again so wildly that he grew scared, wrenched himself loose and said: "There are a few difficulties. You know that." Then he went.

I'm alone now. I've locked myself in. I've barricaded the door so that they can't get in to me—none of them. Now I really am alone, and I'll defend myself. I'll look for my cat, talk to Claudia, issue a writ against Verrus, and look for a miracle, look for everything.

Write:[1]

God is Mercy. Why are there drunks?

[1] The text which now follows is clearly in a different hand. Pilate dictated it to his slave. By this time the former Governor's mind was quite unhinged. I questioned the slave, a certain Eleazar. He admitted that on earlier occasions he had noticed signs of insanity in his master. He had, he assured me, always been of a different opinion from that of his master with regard to the State and the person of the Emperor. In reply to my question as to whether he had taken down the dictation word for word he agreed that it was possible that he had made one or two mistakes. Although he doesn't actually make a bad impression it is not easy to sum up this slave. He is an active Christian. L.P.B.

I believe in the Holy Spirit. Why don't Christians believe in the Holy Spirit?

Jesus has risen from the dead. Why doesn't he take my pen and write: "Pilate wants to be a good man"? They say that it's beautiful in Heaven. Why don't I believe that? Why do I believe in a Heaven in which they beat me? If there's a God, why does he go to sleep? If I don't even understand him, will he understand me? And why? Because he is God? Does he understand everything on that account? Why does he understand the Emperor's pseudo-piety and Stephanio's venality, but not the sufferings of my cat? Because there is no justice on earth? Why is there no justice on earth?

Because if there were there would be no need for a Heaven.

Of course God understands the sufferings of my cat. He just does nothing to alleviate them, that's all.

Why doesn't he?

Because he's God.

So he's a God because he doesn't alleviate suffering.

March 18th.

Injustice is being done to me.

They want to poison me.

They have already poisoned my wife, drowned my cat, and stolen my money.

And I know who did it too.

They sit in the Temple and sing hymns, and you'd think butter wouldn't melt in their mouths.

I am a Christian.

I am not a Christian.

But I have dreams such as no one has ever had before

and no one will ever have again: big, significant dreams.

March 24th.

There is music in the air.
The music is whining—like cats.
The Emperor is an honourable man.
He murders according to the law.
He has done me a great injustice.
He wants to get rid of me; he too.
Because I know that there is music in the air: cater-wauling: high, clear, pervasive tones—and a great deal of mist.

March 30th.

The Christian God came. He just wanted to pay me a visit, he said.

He poured out wine for me, and that made me think immediately that he wanted to poison me too, so I let him drink first; which he did. Strange! All the same, I must be careful. To make conversation I asked him how his son was.

"They crucified him," he replied.

I told him I was sorry about that, and then I asked him how he was. "Not so good," he replied.

"That's a pity," I said.

April 6th.

Write:

Diogenes drank the hemlock. Socrates lived in a tub. Jesus died in the fight for freedom against Rome. Pilate was crucified. The Emperor prays. God languishes.

A priest cut off Seneca's ear. It lies in the street and twitches. Laughter can be heard from the underworld.

251

Socrates washes his hands in innocence. There are beetles in the head. The murderers of Pilate look as though butter wouldn't melt in their mouths. Foaming at the mouth is better than praying. There are beetles in the head. At night they shine. And hurt.

Where is my cat?